Her eyes met his, finally.

He ran his fingertips where her dimples showed when she smiled. Bree wasn't smiling now. "Why are you sorry?"

"Because I have feelings for you. Because I'm leaving soon."

Hearing her admit she cared did something to him. Something he didn't expect. Something he didn't want to lose. "Do you really have to go way out to Seattle?"

"Don't even think of asking me to stay."

He didn't want to let this die, but then, what kind of chance did they have? "We can keep in touch."

That sounded lame, even to his ears. They'd known each other a couple of weeks but it was long enough to have feelings for each other. Real feelings he should know better than to pursue. Hadn't he learned that whirlwind romances didn't last?

Glancing at Bree's hand wrapped firmly in his own made him wonder if maybe they could—with the right woman.

Bree was real and she cared. Problem was, he didn't want her to leave. But if he asked her to stay, he might lose her forever.

Jenna Mindel lives in northwest Michigan with her husband and their three dogs. A 2006 Romance Writers of America RITA® Award finalist, Jenna has answered her heart's call to write inspirational romances set near the Great Lakes.

Books by Jenna Mindel

Love Inspired

Maple Springs

Falling for the Mom-to-Be
A Soldier's Valentine
A Temporary Courtship

Big Sky Centennial

His Montana Homecoming

Mending Fences
Season of Dreams
Courting Hope
Season of Redemption
The Deputy's New Family

A Temporary Courtship

Jenna Mindel

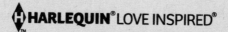
HARLEQUIN® LOVE INSPIRED®

Recycling programs for this product may not exist in your area.

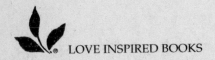

LOVE INSPIRED BOOKS

ISBN-13: 978-0-373-81940-9

A Temporary Courtship

www.Harlequin.com

Printed in U.S.A.

Then the LORD God said,
"It is not good that the man should be alone;
I will make him a helper fit for him."
—*Genesis* 2:18

To my husband, for supporting my dream.
I love you!

Chapter One

Conservation officer Darren Zelinsky blew out his breath and stared at the Bay Willows Association community building. He'd been here more times than he cared to remember with Raleigh, the woman he'd once planned to marry. He wasn't here today by choice either.

Bay Willows was a private summer resort located within his hometown of Maple Springs, Michigan. The large white two-story Victorian structure before him, complete with a broad porch on one side, reminded him of what he'd lost. And what he hoped to gain by coming here.

Ice cream socials were held on that porch. The last time he'd been to an ice cream social two years ago with his girl, it had taken every ounce of willpower to play nice with people he'd resented since he was kid. People who'd looked down their noses at a local, making him feel like an awkward teen trying to protect his turf.

Darren had Local Yokel stamped on his forehead, and that wasn't ever going to change. He didn't want it to. He loved not only Maple Springs but also the entire Tip of the Mitt. It was why he was so good at his job with the state's Department of Natural Resources.

The late April afternoon had turned warm and sunny. A perfect day for mushrooming. Teri, his supervisor, had asked him to fill in for her wild edibles class. This wasn't for fun, it was work. This was the opportunity he needed, too, because he wanted her job.

Rumor had it that Teri might not return from maternity leave with her late-in-life surprise baby. He'd also heard that her husband relocated to the town they'd come from downstate. Good news for Darren. He didn't want to come in second place this time. The supervisor job should have been his over two years ago, but his regional boss had gone with Teri instead, a more seasoned CO several years older than Darren. Teri was used to dealing with a more diverse population.

He glanced around the area he'd avoided for nearly two years. He had to prove himself here. Prove he had what it took to get along with these people. But so many bad memories resided here, alongside these beautiful people.

Most cottages remained shut up for winter. The majority of summer residents arrived in time for Memorial Day, a month away yet. Summertime in Maple Springs was gorgeous, but with the beauty came the crowds. His town swelled with part-timers and tourists overtaking the shops and sidewalks and slowing down traffic.

Bay Willows threw open her gates on April 1. Half a dozen or so of those early residents had signed up for this class. Every week for the next few, Darren would instruct uppity summer residents how not only to prepare but also to find wild edibles. He was more than qualified. He'd been scouring the woods since he was a kid. He knew where to find everything Teri had planned before her doctor called her out.

Farm to table was big right now, and foraging for local fare had become an *in* thing. If there was one thing he'd learned about Bay Willows, being *in* was important. Darren had never been one for fads or passing fancies. Safety was his thing. Protecting the area he loved.

But God had a funny way of making a man face his past. And his failures. So here Darren stood in front of the Bay Willows community building, a place he'd vowed never to step foot in again, hoping to somehow rewind history. He wanted a different outcome this time. He'd not only get the job he wanted but also get over Raleigh, banishing her from his soul so he could move on.

She wouldn't be here. She'd hated these kinds

of things, calling the classes and workshops given by Bay Willows "hokey gatherings for bored housewives and grandmothers." She'd had a rebellious streak when it came to this place, disdaining it almost as much as he. Maybe that was what had made him attractive to her in the first place. He didn't belong here and Raleigh knew that, but he hadn't been good enough to keep. In the end, she'd left him.

Music tugged his attention away from his dark thoughts. String music. A violin?

"Good. Now pick up the pace. Like this," a woman's voice, muffled and barely discernible, encouraged.

He heard a deeper string sound emanate from above, streaming out an open second-floor window like a soft spring rain. Mellow and warm, the song wrapped around him. For a moment, he forgot why he didn't want to be here. Even his plan to go over the class notes one more time faded away as he simply listened.

The violin joined in, trying to keep up. Whoever played the deeper sounding instrument was good. Really good. The music suddenly stopped, followed by the scrape of a chair. "Sorry, but I've got to run." A pause and then, "Let me know if you need help."

He couldn't hear the response. Whoever played the violin kept going, but the richer-sounding instrument was done. *Bummer*. It wasn't a bass. What were those things called...

Darren shifted his satchel and focused on the double doors ahead. Time to go to work. He took one more sweeping look around the clump of a few buildings that made up the Bay Willows administrative campus in the midst of summer cottages arranged by the lake. Confident his ex-fiancée wasn't lurking in the shadows, Darren stepped inside.

The community room had a kitchen where he'd demonstrate how to prepare what they found in the field. He took over a table at the front of the main room and pulled out the required paperwork. Liability waivers, emergency contact information and wild edible booklets for each attendee along with a calendar of class topics and a list of suggested items to bring on each outing. He was as ready as he'd ever be.

"Mr. Zelinsky?"

He jerked his head up at the sound of a feminine voice. "Yes?"

A slight woman with dark brown hair framing a pretty face stood before him, scattering his thoughts. She was average height but delicate-looking; her full lips stained red made her creamy skin look that much lighter. Her bangs had been cut short and jagged as if she'd let a kid loose with scissors. His sisters had had dolls with choppy bangs like that by the time they'd gotten done with them. The rest of the woman's thick hair was long and straight.

Her eyes were a wild golden color framed by dark lashes, putting him in mind of the bobcat he'd come upon last winter. No eye makeup, as far as he could tell; she didn't need it. She stepped closer and held out her hand. "Bree Anderson. My mother, Joan, organized this class, but she's off her feet with a broken ankle, so I'm here to help."

Momentarily mesmerized by those eyes, he didn't take her offered hand. "Help?"

She looked at him like he might be dim-witted—the typical local boy without a brain. "You know, help with anything you may need since you're sort of filling in at the last minute."

He'd had a good week's notice. Plenty of time. "What did you say your name was?"

"Bree. Bree Anderson." She let her hand drop.

On the edge of uppity, the name suited her. Bree Anderson looked exactly like what he'd expect. *Pampered*, *sheltered* and *expensive* were written all over her.

"Like the cheese?" He threw out that verbal jab without thinking.

Amusement shone from Bree's eyes instead of offense. Her mouth lifted, making deep dimples in her cheeks. One more thing to tease him. "Yes. Exactly like the cheese but with two *e*'s and no *i*."

She had a slight lilt in her voice. Not a prominent accent or anything, simply a different way of enunciating certain words that made it obvious she wasn't from around here.

"Got it. My name's Darren." He handed over the forms. She'd be his liaison, then, the link between a backward local and the *in* summer folk. "You might as well read and sign these. Everyone needs to complete them before we go anywhere. Let me know if you have any questions."

"Sure thing." She bit the top of the pen as she read over the forms. Straight white teeth were framed by those full, bow-shaped red lips. Who wore red lipstick?

Who cared? He liked it.

Tightening his jaw, he turned away. He needed to stop noticing things about her, now. Noticing led to attraction, and that could only lead to trouble. Darren had had enough trouble with one woman from Bay Willows to last a lifetime.

Bree signed her name in a tight scrawl and handed over the waiver. "Seems self-explanatory. Seek and eat at our own risk."

"Exactly." He took the signed forms without looking at her.

"Darren, is that you?"

His heart pitched when he heard that voice. Of course Raleigh's grandmother would sign up. She lived here during the open months of April through November when she wasn't in Florida. "It's me. How are you, Stel?"

"I didn't know you'd be teaching this class. The confirmation letter had a woman's name on it." Stella hustled toward him for a big hug.

He returned it, of course. He'd always liked Raleigh's grandmother. She'd treated him well and had referred to him as her new favorite grandson. She'd accepted him as-is—the only one of them who'd done so.

"Teri went out early on maternity leave," Darren explained.

"Oh." Stella's gaze narrowed. "Bree! I didn't expect to see you here. Do you two know each other?"

"We just met." Bree smiled.

"Oh, well, good. That's good." Stella's penciled-in eyebrows arched toward her hairline. "How's your mom?"

"She needs to stay off her feet for a while, but she'll be fine."

"Fortunate for all of us. Yes, very fortunate." Stella glanced from him to Bree and then back to him. "Joan broke her ankle playing tennis. Can you imagine?"

There were worse things broken in life, but Darren didn't say that. He nodded as he watched more people enter the room. Mostly women, but a couple of men joined them, too. All of them looked well beyond retirement age. Could these people safely tromp around in the woods? He'd find out soon enough.

* * *

Bree listened to the DNR guy, Darren, introduce himself and explain the scope of the class. There were ten students, including her. She recognized several but didn't really know anyone except for Stella. They'd often shared a practice room back in the day when Stella played the violin. Bree had given her a few lessons and had loved their time together. What the woman lacked in skill, she more than made up for in flamboyant kindness.

Bree spotted the wire mesh basket in Stella's hands. Everyone else had a container or bag of sorts. The two men each had green net bags like the ones her avocados came in. All her mother had told her was that they'd meet here, go foraging and then come back to the community room for a quick demonstration on cleaning and preparing what they'd found. She hadn't considered bringing a container.

But then, that was a logical deduction and Bree wasn't exactly into logic. She believed people could change, when in reality they couldn't or wouldn't. Not to mention, she'd been told a thousand times that her head was too filled with notes and chords to return the milk to the fridge.

Bree scanned the paper calendar. She looked forward to today's hunt for black morels. Next week was ramps—whatever those were—and fiddlehead ferns. Her stomach turned at the last one. Memories of an argument over trying something as harmless as fiddlehead ferns rang through her thoughts. She should have ended it with Philip back then.

She zeroed in on wild asparagus in a class three weeks from now. She'd never realized her favorite vegetable could be found out in the wild. She'd assumed it was grown in gardens, having only purchased it in a grocery store.

Bree had never had a garden of her own. She wouldn't have begun to know what to do with one. Hours of daily practice on the cello had been a priority all her life. She'd missed out on a few things. Maybe a lot of things, but she wouldn't trade her music for anything. Or anyone. She'd realized that almost too late.

She wouldn't miss out today. This class promised something different than her usual routine. Right now, Bree craved different. For the first time in a long while, she felt free. Free to do whatever she wanted before following her dreams. A few weeks of relative leisure before the hard work began. Toiling under the tutelage of an orchestral composer for the next two years was a dream come true and one that would require all her focus.

"If no one has any questions about the paperwork, I'll collect it now, and then we can head out."

Bree snapped out of her thoughtful haze,

helped gather up the signed waivers and handed them to Darren. "Here."

"Thank you." He gave her a tight nod, barely looking at her.

Bree couldn't help but look at him, though. His fingers were bare of any rings, and he had light brown hair that curled even though he kept it short. Despite the gray-green uniform he wore, she pictured him as a flannel shirt kind of guy. Like the lumberjack on those paper towel commercials. The breadth of Darren's shoulders hinted that he might not be a stranger to chopping wood.

Her pulse skittered when he caught her staring. His eyes were blue—bright blue and wary.

Bree smiled, hoping he understood that she meant no harm. She'd recently broken up with a man who'd nearly robbed her of her dreams. She wasn't about to risk another relationship that might trap her where she and her music had no place to grow.

"Let's load up." Darren made his way to the door as if he couldn't get out fast enough. Away from her.

Bree laughed under her breath. Was she scary? All she'd done was smile. Okay, maybe she'd checked him out thoroughly. But who'd blame her? He was a good-looking guy. Not that she'd do anything about it. She wasn't even window-shopping.

But if she were...

Another laughable thought. Still, Darren Zelinsky made for one very handsome display.

"Come on, honey. This is going to be fun." Stella patted her arm.

Bree had a feeling that might be true, but her curiosity had been piqued. "So, what's his story?"

"Darren?" Stella shook her head and whispered, "I'll tell you later. Come for dinner?"

Imaginings of a sordid, operatic tale tickled her curiosity. Bree wanted to know more. She leaned close. "I'd love to."

Stella wrapped her arm around Bree and squeezed. "You know my door's always open. Tonight we can cook up what we find."

Bree giggled. Something she did little of but always with Stella. "Sounds like a good plan."

"My plans are always good ones." Stella winked and headed out the door.

Bree dashed back into the kitchen for a couple of plastic storage bags to gather up those morel mushrooms. The last one finally to leave the building, she squinted at the sudden brightness outside. Three in the afternoon on the last Tuesday in April and the weather was perfect. The sun finally shone between puffy white clouds after a couple of days of gray rain.

Bree noted that everyone had already loaded up and waited for her to get in the van. Her stomach clenched. Did DNR Darren mind that she'd held them up? He didn't look too pleased.

The only seat left was the front passenger seat, next to him. She climbed in and glanced his way, but he was busy counting heads.

When he finished, she asked, "So, where are we going?"

"State land not far out of town." He didn't sound annoyed and concentrated on backing out.

Breathing easier, she asked more questions. "Do these black mushrooms grow out in the open?"

"In the woods."

"Oh." She glanced at her brand-new light gray flats and frowned.

Obviously she hadn't dressed right, but then, she wasn't an outdoorsy kind of gal. Her idea of a hike was walking the shoreline here or her parents' neighborhood in Royal Oak. It wasn't that she didn't like it outside, but living in Detroit didn't exactly invite running wild outdoors. She'd spent a lot of time inside practicing, where her imagination ran wild within the confines of a music room.

She noticed Darren's hands as he gripped the steering wheel. They were strong hands with scrapes and calluses. Nothing like the spotless manicured hands belonging to Philip. Darren was very different from the professionally polished man she'd dated far too long.

Another bomb she'd soon drop on her parents. She'd not only quit her position with the symphony to accept a music residency out west but also discarded her parents' chosen husband for her. The seemingly perfect man, but Bree knew better. He wasn't perfect for her.

The chatter and laughter behind them grew louder as they turned off a main road onto a dirt one. Bouncing along, Bree grabbed the handle on the door and glanced at Darren. His face looked carved out of stone. Obviously *he* wasn't having fun.

"Do you do this often?"

"What?"

"Give these kind of classes."

"This is my first." He drove slower and concentrated on the pathway ahead. He took another turn onto what couldn't really be called a road but had tracks proving vehicles had traveled it before.

Real chatty guy.

Bree bit her bottom lip and stared out the window. It was pretty here in the woods. The tender green leaves were just beginning to unfurl, way behind the spring growth downstate. She spotted a small tree with buds bursting into a white flower here and there. "What's that tree blooming over there?"

Darren looked where she pointed. "Juneberry tree."

"Oh."

"The fruit is edible."

"So, where'd you learn all this?"

Darren shrugged as he took another turn. "My grandmother taught me what to look for when I was a kid."

Bree melted when she thought of this big, gruff man as a small boy following his grandmother around, learning about wild food and where to find it. "Neat."

He grunted agreement, slowed the van to a stop and turned in his seat toward the passengers in the back. "After you get out, please stay near the van for instructions."

Amid grumbles from one of the elderly men, Bree peered through the windshield. They'd stopped in a small clearing surrounded by trees. The vehicle path went deeper into the woods, but evidently they were here, wherever here was. And it was bound to get interesting scouring the area with this group of rowdy seventy-year-olds.

Bree turned when she felt a pat on her shoulder. Looking into Stella's eyes, she chuckled when the elderly woman wiggled her eyebrows. As if she and Darren had hit it off. More like she'd made him angry, considering the way he barked orders.

She glanced at him, shocked to find him watching her. "What?"

"You getting out?"

Of course she was getting out. What did he

think, after they'd come all this way she'd stay in the van? "Yes. Why?"

"No reason." He shrugged and exited the vehicle.

Bree watched him walk around the front. He tapped lightly on the hood as if dreading this. She knew irritation when she saw it. What was his problem, anyway?

Bree pocketed her phone and grabbed her bag. Maybe she should try to find out.

Chapter Two

Darren glanced at Bree as she slid from the passenger seat of the van, and he shook his head. She was dressed in light-colored cropped pants and shoes that were barely more than slippers. He'd be surprised if she stayed clean. Unless she was the prissy type that wouldn't get her hands dirty. She'd go home empty-handed if that were true.

She looked nothing like his ex-girlfriend, but Bree came from the same place. Overdressed for roaming around outside, she might as well have been cut from the same cloth as Raleigh.

He had ten people to look after. He needed to quit focusing on one. It was up to him to show them respect for the woods. And that meant staying alert. "Gather around, please."

Darren passed out plastic whistle lanyards to each person as they stepped close. "Stay in pairs at all times, and if you get turned around, just blow your whistle. I'll find you."

He waited for them to slip the whistles over their heads, and then he held up the wild edibles pamphlet. "Open your booklet to page three, and take a good look at the picture of the morel mushroom. Notice the pattern and the shape, with the bottom closed around the stem. That's what we're looking for. Stay away from the blobby-looking ones. They're false morels. There are also caps that are open on the bottom like an umbrella. They're edible, but use caution. They make some people sick. I'll go through what you find before we leave to make sure they're all safe. Any questions?"

Stella raised her hand.

"Stel?"

"We shouldn't eat them now, right?" She knew that but was trying to help him out.

He hadn't even thought about mentioning it and appreciated the reminder. These people didn't know what they were doing. This was a novelty. A vacation treat. "Right. They need to be cleaned of grit, and there might be a rare stowaway bug inside. Morels are way better cooked, in my opinion. I'll show you how to clean them when we return." He checked his watch. "Okay, we'll meet back here in forty-five minutes."

"Darren, will you find the first morel for us before we split up?" Stella asked.

He noticed everyone nodding in agreement. Okay, maybe he wasn't so good at leading this class. They had no clue what to look for and where. He'd almost sent them away without showing them. All because he'd been in a hurry to get rid of them. Especially Bree.

He gestured for them to follow and headed for a wooded area, keeping his gaze focused on the ground. "They're dark, a blackish-tan triangle. Look around these ash trees. See the gray bark?"

He noticed that Bree watched his every move and copied it. She bent down low but didn't touch anything. "Oh! Is this one?"

He leaned close to her, still bent over and staring at the ground. He could smell her perfume, or maybe it was her shampoo. Whatever it was, it stopped him cold like a sucker punch to the gut. The soft, flowery scent teased his senses and begged him to move closer.

He didn't.

He couldn't go there. Some things might smell good at first but ended up rotten. Spoiled rotten. He'd found that out much too late.

He took a knee and waited for the rest of the class to gather round. "This is exactly what we're looking for. Morels. Take care where you step and look around. Where there's one, there are bound to be more. Pinch off the stem so the roots stay in the ground. Like this."

He offered the mushroom to Bree.

"I get the first one?" Her fingertips grazed his palm as she scooped it up and dropped it into her plastic bag.

"You found it."

She grinned at him. Proud of herself.

Another sucker punch. The jaws of attraction snapped around him like a rusty old trap digging in deep. He couldn't let it poison his blood. Or his brain by giving it room to grow.

"Here are some!" one of the women announced, not far away.

Darren stopped staring at Bree and jogged over to inspect the finding. Sure enough, his class was on a roll as another morel was found, then another. "Good job. I think everyone's got it."

He pulled a small red onion bag from his pocket and joined the hunt.

"Why that kind of bag?" Bree came up from behind him. She had several mushrooms bulging from the bottom of her plastic grocery store variety.

"It lets the spores fall and reseed."

"Oh." She didn't wander far from his side.

Why'd she stick with him? He'd hoped she would have joined Stella's group of three ladies. He heard laughter and shouts as more found mushrooms, and Darren silently thanked the Lord for small favors. They hadn't been skunked on his first class.

"Should I pick these little ones?" Bree asked.

He stepped closer. They were small white morels yet to mature. "Go ahead. They'll get picked by somebody else if you leave 'em."

"So, people come way out here?"

He nodded. "A lot of people. I've run into campers from downstate, Ohio, even Indiana, up here picking on state land. Gather as much as they can to enjoy or sell."

"I've had morels before at a golf club dinner but never gave much thought to where they came from."

Local ingredients were desirable, and some of the finer restaurants in town paid top dollar to serve local morels. Darren didn't frequent those places anymore. The places Raleigh had dragged him to. Give him plain cooking at Dean's Hometown Grille in town any day. But his breakup had chased him from going there. Too many sympathy glances and gossip.

After Raleigh left him, Darren didn't go anywhere he might run into her. He'd stayed away from downtown Maple Springs, where she lived with his best friend, Tony. He'd stayed away from Bay Willows and the memories there, too. In fact, he pretty much stayed away from women in general. Too often they tried to turn him into someone he wasn't, like Raleigh had. She'd told him that he'd never change and was stuck in a rut doing the same thing all the time.

Maybe that was true, but Darren loved what he did. He'd grown up here, where the summer residents and tourists bloated the population from a mere two thousand to ten times that number, crowding out those who lived here year-round. Some of his friends had tried to emulate them in manner and dress. Tony had been one of them. Never content to embrace where he came from, Tony wanted more. Tony wanted too much and took more than he should have.

Darren glanced at Bree and spotted a mushroom at her feet. He bent to pluck it. If she wanted to know where morels came from, today's outing answered it. A person couldn't put a price tag on finding these. "They come from right here."

"I almost stepped on that one." She laughed and kept walking forward, slow and hunched over. Her hair fell like a curtain, draping her face from view. Her gray slip-ons were dirty at the toes, and her pants had streaks of dirt on them, too. She wore a gold-colored windbreaker that made her easy to spot. That color also made her eyes glow. Like a cat's eyes.

Darren wasn't real fond of cats. Even his parents' cat drove him nuts with all its hollering for attention, only to run away if he tried to pet it. Women were like cats in that way. He preferred dogs. Dogs didn't tease.

"Ooh, here's another couple." She picked them

properly and foraged on, poking her fingers under dead leaves and raking through the clumps of grass here and there.

Well, she wasn't prissy. He'd give her that. He found a few more as well and checked his watch. Twenty minutes to go. He stood and glanced around the woods. Stella was out of sight, as were several others, but he heard lots of chatter. No one lost. That was good. Real good.

"So, what does a DNR officer do besides take a bunch of us resorters out in the woods to look for food?"

Resorters. Even that sounded pretentious.

"As a conservation officer," he corrected her, "my job is to provide natural resources protection and ensure recreational safety, as well as provide general law enforcement duties."

"That sounds like it came right out of a textbook."

"It did." Straight out of his employee handbook.

She smiled, causing those delectable dimples to reappear. "Do you like what you do?"

Here we go. The usual female digging. At first, Raleigh had liked the idea of what he did for a living—the whole man-in-uniform-with-a-gun thing. But then the limitations of his pay coupled with his desire to stay put in Northern Michigan had bothered her. Obviously too much. He should have believed her when she'd said she wanted to travel and eventually move away to a more urban area.

"I love my job." Darren didn't want to do anything else but grow within this region and climb the short ladder right here.

Bree nodded. "That's good."

Curious, he asked her the same. "What about you?"

"I play the cello."

The cello. That was the instrument whose name he couldn't remember. He stopped walking. "Hey, so that was you practicing before class."

Bree grinned. "It was. Along with a woman who plays the violin in a string quartet here. There are practice rooms above the community room. Bay Willows is hoping to start a summer music school. They've bought up a couple of vacant cottages near the community building, but I suppose you know that."

"I didn't." Something like that would only bring more people here. "You're good."

"I know." There was no bragging in her voice. She'd stated a simple fact. Like any professional acknowledging a skill level.

"Do you give lessons, then?"

She spotted another morel and picked it. "Not really. I'm not into teaching little kids how to play, you know? I play with the Detroit Symphony Orchestra—well, I used to."

"Used to?"

"I quit."

He stared at her. She obviously wanted him to ask the reason, and the funny thing was, Darren wanted to know. "Okay. Why?"

"Last year, I applied for a two-year music residency that would encompass composing. I'd like to compose. And, well, recently I got called and accepted." She let out a deep breath. "There, practice before delivery speech."

He didn't want to go there, but something about the vulnerable look in her eyes made him probe. "Is it a secret?"

"No. I've wanted to work under a composer for years, but I haven't ever had the chance before. My parents don't know yet, but then, it came together pretty fast."

She looked old enough to make her own decisions. "And they'll have a problem with it?"

Bree shrugged. There was obviously more to her story, but all she said was, "I'll find out."

He nodded and they fell silent, each one searching out mushrooms in opposite directions. After several minutes, he stood, stretched and spotted Bree a few yards away.

Her eyes were closed, her head tilted toward the sky. Her dark brown hair blazed with coppery color where the sun hit it.

His gut tightened. He didn't want to care about why this woman worried over her parents' reaction. He didn't want to like her at all, but there was something about her that tugged at him. Like a rare wildflower that needed protection from getting picked.

At that moment, she opened her eyes, looked right at him and grinned. "I was listening to the sounds of the woods."

He cocked his head. What was she talking about?

"You know, the birdsong and the breeze rustling those crepe-paper-looking leaves on those little trees over there." She wasn't putting him on.

"I can't remember what they are. Some kind of aspen, maybe." He wished he knew. He'd look it up.

"Interesting sounds out here."

"Haven't you been in the woods before?"

"I've summered here most of my life, but I've never ventured far from the main thoroughfares. Maybe Traverse City or Mackinac Island."

He shook his head. "You're missing the best parts of Northern Michigan."

She turned interested eyes on him. "So, where are these best parts?"

He took the bait. "Open fields with hills rising behind them. A twisting river loaded with brookies. The Pigeon River Forest where elk roam. Come winter, there are awesome snowmobile trails, pine trees heavy with snow and blue moonlight."

She gave him an odd look. "You sound like a poet."

Darren kicked at the ground cover. He'd gotten carried away. "I appreciate the area, is all."

"No desire to live elsewhere?"

"None." He was a local. He'd always be a local even though he'd been an army baby. His mother had moved him and his brother Zach permanently to Maple Springs after their brother Cam was born. She'd wanted her kids to have a home, an anchor. Some of his siblings had flown far from the nest after high school, but Darren wasn't a traveler. He'd gone to college only a couple hours away before attending conservation officer training academy.

The people who summered at Bay Willows came from all over. Mainly the Midwest, sure, but most were well-traveled and liked to tell where they'd been. They peppered their conversation with travel itineraries the way folks in old movies plastered travel stickers on their suitcases. Raleigh used to tease that he was backward, having never really been anywhere as an adult.

"Hmm." Bree's attention zeroed in on the ground. "Oh, here are some more."

Glad for the distraction, Darren let the matter drop, because it didn't matter. Bree Anderson was both educated and no doubt well-traveled. She was accustomed to a lifestyle he'd never had and never would have. With the supervisor position came a pay increase that would be more than enough for him. He didn't care about making scads of money.

If Bree found him interesting, it was only temporary. He wasn't the kind of guy a girl like Bree would keep for the long haul. Darren wasn't good enough for the Bay Willows crowd. He'd learned that lesson pretty well. Darren only had to make a mistake once to know he'd never repeat it.

On the drive back to Maple Springs, Bree peered into her plastic grocery sack at the pile of blackish-tan edibles heaped there. She breathed in the soft, earthy smell of fungi. Nothing too strong or pungent, she had trouble coming up with a comparison for the aroma. She'd picked these delicacies in the woods, with her own two hands.

How cool.

"How many do you have?" Darren's voice sounded awfully gentle for such a gruff guy.

"Uh." Bree looked up. She sat up front again, in the passenger seat. "I don't know."

Darren's mouth curved into a half smile. "Considering how long you were staring into that bag, I thought you were counting them."

"Nope, just smelling them." She didn't want

to explain what a novel experience this had been for her. Different than what she was used to and, well, it had been fun. Really fun. But more importantly, it had made her feel strong. Capable. Empowered?

Okay, maybe that went too far.

He chuckled, the sound a soft rumble from within his chest. Maybe he wasn't as gruff as he pretended to be.

Bree's phone whistled with an incoming text, and she pulled it from her coat pocket. Briefly she closed her eyes after she'd read the name. That made three this week. "Excuse me."

"No problem."

Call me when you get a chance. Want to see how you're doing. Philip.

Bree had no intention of calling him. Instead, she replied with a text.

I'm fine. Helping with one of my mom's classes. Thanks.

She scanned two previous messages that were similar. One had been Philip checking that she'd made it safely to her parents' summer cottage. She was okay with that one, but the next two? Really, Philip needed to let it go. He needed to let *her* go.

Bree slipped the phone back into her pocket as the van pulled up to the community building. Clutching her cache of mushrooms, she got out with the rest of the group and headed inside.

"Gather in the kitchen and I'll show you how to clean and cook the morels," Darren called.

"I know how to cook mushrooms." The grumbly guy named Ed had a decidedly sharp tone.

Bree glanced at Darren. He looked calm enough despite the flush of red that tipped his ears.

"We all do. In fact, you can prepare morels any way you'd normally cook or sauté other mushrooms. Personally, I like to bread mine. It's no problem if you prefer not to stick around."

Bree looked back at Ed.

The old guy wasn't appeased by Darren's offer to leave. "Now look here—"

"I'd like to know how you cook them," Bree quickly interrupted.

Others agreed. Situation diffused.

Bree relaxed as the tension eased and Ed nodded for Darren to continue. As if he was somehow in charge.

Darren had been beyond patient when they'd run late because there were so many mushrooms to find and pick. No one had wanted to leave. Including Bree. Who'd have guessed she'd enjoy roaming the woods so much? She didn't even care that her shoes were dirty or her pants filthy from wiping her fingers on them.

Darren showed that same patience now in the face of Ed's belligerence as he emptied his morels into a bowl in the sink. "Cleaning is easy. Just soak them in salt water, swish them around a bit, and then rinse and drain like so. Get as much water off as you can. Then you're ready to cook."

Bree watched as he laid the washed mushrooms out on paper towels. And the questions started to fly.

"Can you dry them for storing?"

"Yes."

"How?"

"String them up to air-dry or use the lowest setting on a dehydrator. I've seen them laid out on an old window screen in the sun to dry."

That got their class buzzing with chatter.

"What about freezing?" another asked.

"Freeze after drying, or freeze after sautéing. If you freeze after picking, don't wash them. If they're wet you'll ruin them."

Bree nearly laughed at Darren's clipped answers. He looked like a man who wanted out of there. His earlier patience had worn thin. She watched as he quickly melted a huge glob of butter in a frying pan before dredging the mushrooms in a flour mixture. He threw the coated morels in the pan.

The group murmured likes and dislikes while

the intoxicating smell of melted butter and sizzling mushrooms teased Bree's senses. Her stomach grumbled in response.

"Not good for my diet," one of the ladies said.

Several agreed. But Bree didn't care. Those things looked and smelled delicious.

"What's that mixture you use?" Ed sounded almost polite. Not quite, but still.

Darren took his time answering, turning the morels over in the pan. "Flour, salt and pepper. Seasoned salt works, too."

Bree scanned their group huddled around the island waiting as Darren ladled those butter-fried mushrooms onto a paper towel–lined plate.

He lifted the plate to share. "Be careful. They're hot."

In this batch, there were enough mushrooms for everyone to try a couple. Bree waited till the end before she took her two. The anticipation was worth it. She closed her eyes while savoring the buttery, mild mushroom taste.

"Well?" He tipped his head. Did he really want to know what she thought?

Bree soaked his interest up like a sponge. "Firm texture and subtle flavor. These are really good."

Darren smiled. Big and broad like his shoulders.

And Bree was momentarily stunned. At a loss for words, all because of one smile from one interesting, burly man sharing a moment, an actual connection with her—over cooked mushrooms!

She popped the last morel into her mouth and mumbled, "I've got to run."

Class wrapped up quickly after Bree scurried out. She reminded him of his sisters who'd up and bolt when they'd suddenly remember they left their curling irons plugged in somewhere. But surely that couldn't be it. Bree's hair was straight and shiny. Would that thick mass of mink-colored tresses be soft or coarse to the touch?

He scowled. Not the kind of thoughts he should have.

"What? Did you find some grease that we missed?" Stella and a couple other women had helped him clean up in minutes.

"No. No. It's nothing." He gave them a nod. "Thank you, ladies. Next week, same time and place."

"See you then." Stella walked away and then turned back. "You did a great job today, Darren. Thank you."

Warmth filled him, mixed with shame at spurning her concern this past year. "You're welcome. Good to see you again, Stel."

"And you, as well." She winked and left with her small entourage of elderly friends.

Darren could count on her for good buzz on

his class. Maybe this time around, his regional boss would see that he was ready to deal with anyone. Even the Bay Willows crowd.

When he climbed into the van, he blew out his breath. *Not bad.* His first wild edibles class was done, along with today's shift. And he hadn't run into any problems or his ex. All that stressing over nothing. He'd have to face her one of these days, but not today.

Starting the engine, he checked his rearview mirror, caught a glimpse of a pink-and-green-striped bag on one of the seats and groaned. His day wasn't over yet. He'd have to return that purse to the owner.

He reached back and grabbed it. Hesitating only a moment, he looked inside. Rifling through a woman's purse was not something he relished, but after digging around lipstick tubes and travel packs of tissues, he found a wallet. As he opened that, a driver's license with a picture of Stella greeted him.

At least he knew where she lived. He'd been there many times, with and without Raleigh. He used to stop in to fix a thing or two around Stella's cottage. Who took care of that now? Tony? He doubted that. Tony wasn't exactly a fix-it kind of guy. He'd call a repair man with the excuse that he had more money than time.

Tony knew all about money. From the world of high finance and investments, his best friend had spoken Raleigh's language far better than Darren ever had. The sting of their betrayal still lingered. It wasn't easy to lose his bride and best man in one day—one horrible day that had changed everything.

He pulled into the small driveway of Stella's cottage with the screened-in porch and looked around. No cars were parked nearby other than Stella's little black Buick. He stepped onto the porch. Crisp white wicker furniture with brightly colored cushions had been casually arranged. A vase stuffed with tall, fake flowers stood sentinel on the glass-topped side table.

And this was only the porch.

He finally knocked on the door.

"Darren, what a nice surprise." Stella wore a red-and-white-checkered apron, looking very much like anyone's grandma, only a lot brighter. She applied more makeup than most. "Come in."

He lifted her purse. "I'm just dropping this off. You left it in the van."

"Oh, my. I didn't even miss it. Don't get old." She opened the screen door wide and it squeaked. The thing needed a good dousing of lubricant on the hinges. "Come in for a bit, would you?"

He'd fix the door before he left. Giving Stella a nod he said, "You're not old."

"Thanks, but we both know I am."

He followed Stella into the small summer cottage. She lived alone. Raleigh once said that her husband had died only a couple of years ago.

A lot had happened in those two years. Darren had lost out on his bid for the supervisor position, and then he'd met Stella's granddaughter. It had been a whirlwind romance, one that Darren reeled from still. Memories sliced through him as he walked past the dining room into Stella's kitchen. He could almost hear Raleigh's laughter and the way she'd teased.

It hurt.

"Cookies? I made them this morning."

Darren sat down with a sigh. "Sure."

She patted his shoulder. "How are you?"

"I'm okay." Broken hearts mended with time but never forgot.

"Have you talked to Raleigh?" Stella bustled about the kitchen, stacking cookies on a plate and then pouring him a tall glass of milk.

"Not much to say, is there?"

Stella gave him a long look. "I suppose not."

The question he didn't want to ask nagged like a loose tooth until he finally spit it out. "Is she happy?"

Stella nodded. "She appears to be. Tony's always buying her stuff. His last gift was a diamond ring."

Darren clenched his jaw. He hadn't seen them in months. Nineteen months, three weeks and a few days, to be exact.

She stared him down with a fierce gleam in her eyes. "You're a good man, Darren. Much too good for my granddaughter."

That surprised him, and he grunted around a mouthful of chocolate chip cookie. Stella's granddaughter had stormed into his life and changed it. He'd forever be the spurned groom nearly left at the altar when his bride ran away with his best man after rehearsal. They'd taken off for the honeymoon and had the gall to come back and live under Darren's nose in town. Was it any wonder that people in town looked at him with pity?

He drained his glass and slammed it down on the table. Fortunately, he didn't break the thing, but the loud thwack startled Stella.

He stood. "I'll fix that squeak in your screen door."

Stella smiled up at him. "Do that and I'll make you dinner. I was thinking chicken marsala with those morels we picked. Stay and eat with me."

He looked into her eager face. A few more wrinkles creased around Stella's blue eyes since the last time he'd seen her. For a woman in her early seventies, she was spry. Energetic and a good listener. She'd always been a good listener. Dinner might be a little earlier than he was used to, but food sounded good right now. What harm could there be in staying?

"Okay. I'll stay, on one condition."

"What's that?"

"What else needs fixing around here?"

Stella grinned, obviously pleased. "Well, there is a leaky faucet upstairs."

"Now we're talking." Darren knew where the tools were kept and got to work rummaging for what he'd need. Really, he should have stopped in and checked on Stella sooner.

He could hear her humming while she scattered pots and pans in the kitchen. The phone rang. Stella still had a landline.

"Yup, now's good." Stella's voice dropped to a whisper.

He headed up the stairs so he wouldn't overhear her private conversation. Halfway up, it dawned on him that Stella might be talking to her granddaughter and his gut twisted. Surely, Stella had enough sense not to invite Raleigh over while he was here. He backed down a few steps and strained to listen, but Stella had already hung up the phone.

She was humming again.

Chapter Three

"How was class? Was there a good turnout?" Bree's mother sat on the couch, her broken ankle propped up on a pillow. She wore a soft cast-style boot and had instructions to keep weight off it as much as possible for the next week.

Bree slipped into a pair of loose loafers to match the khakis she'd changed into. "It was good. Including me, there were ten of us. Stella was there."

"How is she?"

"Good. I'm heading over there for dinner."

Her mother frowned. "We've hardly had a chance to talk since you came up. Everything okay?"

Bree hesitated. Really, she was making too much of telling her parents about Philip. About her leaving. "Everything's good. Really good. In fact, I was offered that residency I applied for."

"In Seattle?" Aha, her mother had been paying attention all those months ago. "I thought they chose someone else."

"They did, but something came up and the guy had to decline. I gave notice to the symphony, cleaned out my apartment and shipped out what I'll need. I'll leave here in about a month."

Her mother narrowed her gaze. "What's Philip think about that?"

This was where it got sticky. "We decided to call it quits. It's for the best, all things considered."

"Oh, Bree. He's got a wonderful future ahead of him. You're twenty-nine years old. Isn't it time you stopped studying and settled down?"

Bree had expected that reaction. She'd gone for her master's degree and a couple of short-term fellowships overseas while working her way up to assistant principal cellist. She wasn't ready to get stuck with kids and a husband who'd make demands on her time. She needed to find her real purpose before settling down. Why had she been gifted with the love of music if simply playing was not enough?

Her parents had introduced her to Philip, the son of her father's golf buddy, years ago, with high hopes. Hopes that Bree had shared until she'd applied for the music residency. Philip had been against it from the start, vocalizing that she didn't have a chance. He'd been livid when she went ahead with her application anyway.

She shrugged, sparing her mother the details. "It just didn't work out between us."

"He doesn't want to wait. Two years is a long time, Bree. Maybe you should rethink this residency."

Bree breathed deep. "I've always wanted to try my hand at composing, and this is a prime opportunity."

Her mother didn't understand her restlessness. She'd never understood her desire to be more. Instead of arguing the point, her mother shelved the discussion for later, when she'd have reinforcement from Bree's father. "Well, it's good to have you here for longer than a couple of weeks. You might even catch your sister. She's finally taking some time off and will be up Memorial Day weekend."

Bree bit her lip. Her sister had been the role model in the family. She was a dermatologist married to a doctor with two kids. It didn't get more successful than that in her mother's eyes. "That's great."

Her mother tipped her head. "Thank you for overseeing my class. How'd that officer do? He's filling in, you know. The woman I met with was supposed to facilitate but went out early on maternity leave. And no wonder, considering she's got to be in her forties. See, that could happen to you if you wait too long to have kids. It's a risk, Bree."

She didn't bother addressing that issue. She had plenty of time. Even if she didn't, she'd never been comfortable around small children and wasn't sure she even wanted a family of her own. "So, you haven't met him."

"No. Someone called to tell me about the change a week ago. And then this happened." Her mom lifted her ankle.

"He did a great job. He's knowledgeable." Bree didn't mention that Darren was also attractive and single. Or that Ed had given him grief.

"Well, good. If it's successful, we might offer this class every year."

"I think that's a good idea." Would Darren teach it? If so, she'd be sorry to miss it.

Bree definitely thought this class more fun than most of the interest offerings available through the summer season at Bay Willows. Pottery, painting and bridge were only a few. Her mother, as president of the garden club, had organized the wild edibles course months ago.

"Well, I've got to run. Stella had just started making dinner when I called her. I left a bowl of cleaned morels in the fridge for you and Dad."

"Your father will enjoy them."

She'd split half her bundle with her parents; the other half was going with her. A convenient escape for tonight, but her mother was bound to tell her father the news, and then they'd both sit her down for more information.

Her father would want to know what kind of living she could expect over the next two years. Bree had cashed in her 401(k) to handle incidentals, plus she had a good savings. Room and board were covered in a dorm-like setting as there were other residents working in other areas, but that was pretty much it when it came to compensation.

She had a little over a month up north where troubles melted away in the deep blue waters of Lake Michigan. Only she'd be gone before the lake was warm enough for swimming.

Bree took a deep breath and then let it back out. "Is there anything you need before I go?"

Her mother stared over the rim of her reading glasses and lifted her needlepoint. "I've got this to keep me busy, and your father's outside. I'll be fine."

Her father would be around all week before heading back home to his job in Detroit. He'd make the four and a half-hour trek north to the cottage every weekend, though. Bree had grown up that way. Seeing her father only on weekends during the summer months.

Bree headed out the door. From the front porch, she scanned the gorgeous view of Maple Bay and sighed. The dark blue waters of Lake Michigan slapped rhythmically against the shore while birds sang their hearts out. If only she could capture these sounds and turn them into chords and notes. The view always inspired a chorus in her head. Could sight somehow be translated into sound? A good composer used all the senses.

Could she be good?

She'd written oodles of movements with the hope of putting it all together. One day, she'd hear her own piece played. If she was successful in her residency, others would hear it, too, and she'd finally prove herself capable of not only playing but also creating good string music. She'd rise above the title of simple musician to something special. A real artist.

Bree walked the short couple of blocks away from the shoreline to Stella's cottage, set back against the wooded area. Her stomach dipped when she spotted a big green passenger van with the DNR emblem on the doors. Darren stood on the porch, opening and closing the screen door. Then he went inside.

Bree bit her lip. Maybe he'd only stopped by. And maybe she was acting like a kid with a school yard crush, suddenly afraid to talk to the man. Good grief, she'd see him next week at class and the week after, so what was the big deal?

He was the big deal. Big and strong and attractive, Darren fell on the other side of the bell curve compared to the men she knew. Not that she'd dated all that much before Philip, but she was used to musicians, not strapping outdoorsmen with a chip a mile wide on their broad shoulders.

Walking forward, Bree stepped up onto the screened porch and rapped on the door, then opened it. "Hello?"

Stella hustled down the hallway and waved her in. "Come in the kitchen and you can help me finish dinner."

Bree heard the sound of water running from upstairs followed by a clinking of metal against metal. Then the running faucet again.

"Darren's fixing a couple of things for me. And he's staying for dinner."

"Oh, then I don't want to intrude." Bree backed up a step or two.

"Nonsense." Stella dropped her voice to a whisper. "I purposely left my purse behind so he'd have to stop by. I wanted you two to get to know each other better."

"Stella…" Bree followed her friend into the kitchen.

"Oh, come on. Have a little fun." Stella wiggled her overly penciled eyebrows. "He could use a little female attention."

"Oh? And why is that?" Bree couldn't imagine Darren having any trouble getting a date.

"Broken engagement with my granddaughter. She did the breaking." Stella pursed her lips, obviously not pleased.

"Oh, wow. Darren and Raleigh?" Bree had heard rumors a couple of summers ago about another man. She didn't know Darren was the one who'd been jilted. Betrayed.

Stella nodded. "Be nice to him. That's all I'm saying."

"Stella!" Bree felt for the guy. She really did. It made perfect sense that he'd avoided her. Well, Darren didn't have to worry. Bree had broken it off with Philip because he'd made her choose between him and her music. She couldn't risk another romantic entanglement. No way.

Stella handed her a small cutting board. "He's a good man."

"I'm sure he is—"

"You cut up the morels," Stella interrupted. "I'll get to work on the marsala."

"Okay." She was glad she'd changed topics. Bree knew her way around Stella's kitchen and grabbed a knife. She got to work slicing the rinsed mushrooms, then moved on to making a salad while Stella finished the chicken.

Her thoughts were tied up, trying to remember what she'd heard about Stella's granddaughter. Bree recalled there had been some sort of scandal, something her mother had once said, but Bree hadn't ever paid much attention to the Bay Willows grapevine. Too much fodder to take in.

Footsteps sounded on the wide plank floors, and Bree looked up.

"That smells awe-sssome—" Darren's voice fell away to nothing when he spotted her and frowned.

"Hello." Bree gave him a sheepish smile, feeling like she'd been caught with her hands in the cookie jar—knowing about him and Raleigh.

"Hey."

The wild rabbits that ran around Bay Willows looked less twitchy than this man seeing her here.

"Darren, watch the chicken a minute, would you, while I set the dining room table." Stella exited fast with an arm load of things from the fridge. She was more than a little obvious in leaving them alone.

Bree's cheeks flushed red-hot. "I'm sorry. She invited me, too."

"Nothing to apologize for." Darren stepped close to the stove and stirred the sauce. He turned down the heat. "I hadn't planned to stay, and—"

Horrified, Bree blurted, "You're not going to leave because of me, are you?"

He tipped his head and gave her a cool stare. "What I was going to say is that Stella twisted my arm with the promise of dinner if I fixed the faucet upstairs. Stella's a good cook."

"Oh." Bree relaxed. Sort of. "Sorry."

"Stop saying you're sorry."

"Sorr—I mean, okay." Then she laughed. "It's a habit."

"Saying you're sorry?" Darren didn't look amused by that.

"When I'm nervous, yes." Bree's stomach dropped again. That was a stupid thing to say, but she was used to apologizing to Philip in order to stop an argument before it started.

Darren chuckled. "*You're* nervous?"

Yes. Because you're way too attractive.

Instead of admitting that, Bree squared her shoulders. "Wrong choice of words, perhaps, but I feel like maybe I'm imposing."

"Trust me, you're not."

Silence settled thick between them until he looked around. "Stella? I think it's ready."

"Good. Turn off the heat and put the lid on it." Stella entered the kitchen and foraged in the fridge once more. "What do you two want to drink?"

"Water's fine," Bree said as she ducked out with the salad bowl and set it on the dining room table.

"Same for me." Darren's deep voice sounded a little too loud.

"You're both boring," Stella chirped as she handed over a pitcher of ice-cold water from the fridge. "Now go sit down. I'll bring out the chicken."

Bree remained in the dining room, waiting.

Darren entered and sat down right across from

her, leaving the chair at the head of the table for their host. He looked at her.

She looked back.

Be nice to him. Stella's words roused a nervous laugh Bree choked off before it bubbled out. Darren didn't look like he wanted *nice*. Or anything to do with her, for that matter.

Stella set a large covered dish in the middle of the table. Fragrant steam leaked out, teasing Bree's appetite and stealing her attention.

"Darren, would you mind saying the blessing?" Stella bowed her head.

"Sure." Darren bowed his, too.

Bree followed suit, curious to hear the man pray.

"Bless us, O Lord, and these, Thy gifts, which we are about to receive from Thy bounty. Through Christ, our Lord. Amen."

"Amen," Stella echoed.

Bree glanced at Darren. Did he truly believe? A rote prayer wasn't exactly a blazing emblem of faith, but then she wasn't exactly the pillar of piety, either. Having only come to salvation through Christ recently, Bree had her moments. She was often wrapped up in her own way instead of seeking God's will for her life. But not when it came to her upcoming residency. That was an opportunity, a gift she wouldn't squander.

Darren caught her staring at him and raised his eyebrows in question along with a bowl. "Salad?"

"Yes, please."

"So, Bree, tell us what you've been up to. Darren, did you know she plays the cello?" Stella scooped steaming chicken and sauce-drenched pasta onto her plate. "She used to give me lessons when I played the violin."

Bree smiled. "Say the word and I will again."

Stella patted her hand. "You'd make a great teacher, my dear."

She shook her head. "With adults maybe, but I don't have the patience for kids or beginners."

Darren gave her a nod. "I overheard her play just before class. She's good."

"I'm heading to Seattle at the beginning of June for a two-year residency with a symphony out there. We'll find out if I'm any good at composing."

Stella's eyes widened. "Really? I had no idea. Joan never mentioned anything."

"She didn't know. I just found out, too. I landed this opportunity only because the initial person chosen had a family situation and declined."

"Well, congratulations." Stella smiled.

Bree smiled back. "I'm excited about it."

Darren visibly relaxed. "Two years, huh? Then what?"

Bree shrugged. "I'll find out then. I hope. Working under a composer is something I've dreamed of doing since college. It's really a gift from God."

Darren nodded. "He does that."

That sure sounded like a man of faith talking. "I figured a month up here before leaving might be a good thing. A gift to myself before the hard work begins. Have some fun, you know? Instead of practice, practice, practice."

"Good for you," Stella said.

Bree looked at Darren. "I really enjoyed today's class, by the way. I've never gone off the beaten path into the woods like that. I'm already psyched for next week, looking for fiddleheads."

Darren glanced at Stella.

"See, I told you it was good," Stella said.

Darren shrugged, but those bright blue eyes of his studied Bree. "There's much more than just woods to explore up here."

He'd said that before. "Like blue moonlight?"

"I could show you around some." He looked surprised by his offer.

She was, too, and glanced at Stella.

Be nice to him.

Stella gave her a confident nod, grinning a little too widely. "He knows this area like the back of his hand. You'll be safe, dear, that's for sure."

Safe.

Bree appreciated safety. Knowing Darren was a man of faith and leery of "female attention," as Stella put it, reassured that his offer was not a come-on. DNR Darren wasn't looking for a romantic replacement. Even if he was, Bree already had a position lined up that would take all her energy.

One she wouldn't miss for the world.

Maybe seeing the countryside would inspire her. Something to look back on when things got hard. An intense music residency was bound to get hard, and Bree might need all the inspiration she could get while locked inside for hours on end. Could hanging out with Darren help in some way? After today's outing, she knew it'd be fun.

"You know what? I'll take you up on that offer." Bree nearly laughed at the brief flash of fear that shone from his eyes.

For a split second, Darren looked like he'd jumped in before measuring the depth of a cold lake.

He was handsome, sure, but he had nothing to fear from her. She was safe, too.

Darren couldn't believe he'd just asked this woman out. Maybe not in the conventional sense, but offering to show her what lay off the beaten path might as well have been a date. His grandmother called it courting. He nearly laughed at the thought. He wasn't the get dressed up and bring flowers kind of guy like his grandmother's description of the ideal date. Darren didn't dress up for anyone. Still, Bree surprised him by agreeing to go. He couldn't exactly backpedal his way out of this one without looking like an idiot.

"Where will you take her first?" Stella asked innocently enough, but there was a determined gleam in her eye. She was barking up the wrong tree if she thought to play matchmaker. Hadn't Stella heard? Bree would be gone in a month's time. Gone for two years.

"Not sure." He stalled, and then it dawned on him. "I'm going smelt dipping Friday night with friends. You could come with me."

"What's smelt dipping?" Bree's pretty brow furrowed. Everything about her was pretty. Even the measured way she ate her food was pretty, making sure her pasta was well covered in sauce before taking a bite. She didn't hurry. Refined and polite, she ate slowly.

What would she think about the robust way his family wolfed down a meal? Growing up with six brothers and three sisters, all younger but one, he'd learned to grab food quickly—shovel it in and then go back for seconds before the food was wiped out. Not that Bree would ever meet his family, much less have dinner with them.

Chances were good that if Bree went smelt dipping, she wouldn't like it. Then she might not want to go anywhere else. He'd fulfill his sightseeing offer and that'd be the end of it.

He leaned back in his chair, finished with his dinner. "Smelt are small fish we catch at night with nets. They run into rivers this time of year to spawn."

Bree wrinkled her nose. "I've never fished before."

Genius! He really was a genius at times. He could tell by the pinched look on her face that she wouldn't like it. "It's not real fishing. Not like with a pole, but it's still a good time."

"Hmm. When?"

"We're meeting at the river's edge at nine o'clock, Friday night." He waited for Bree to pass on this opportunity. From her expression, he knew she wasn't interested.

"I'll give it a try."

That answer threw him. She must be serious about trying new things. Only Darren didn't want to be one of those new things. It wasn't as though Bree flirted. Every time he'd looked at her, she'd looked away. And she wasn't shy. Bree had talked her fair share over dinner.

"So, where is this river?"

He glanced at Stella, and it dawned on him that it'd waste time for him to backtrack into town to pick up Bree. He didn't want her getting lost on the way, either, driving by herself. "It's north, nearly to Mackinaw City. We could meet somewhere in between."

Stella paused in sopping up the last of her marsala sauce with a crust of bread. "Why don't you two meet at your house? It's not hard to find and on the way."

Stella had been to his house with Raleigh only once, and yet she remembered the location. Her suggestion made sense, but something about Bree in his home made him squirm.

Bree didn't appear bothered by any of it. She waited for him to respond like it didn't matter to her one way or another. Bree was moving away in a month. Far away, too. Of course it didn't matter where she met him. She wasn't interested in him. He was crazy to think she'd be interested in hanging out with him for some temporary connection before leaving.

"Do you have a piece of paper?" he finally asked.

Stella jumped up and grabbed a notepad and pen, handing it over with a victorious grin.

Darren looked at Bree. She'd finished the last of her salad and then drained her water glass. When she wiped her full-lipped mouth with a napkin, he swallowed hard. A lot could happen in a month.

He concentrated on the paper. "I'll draw you a map. I'm right off the main road, but back in the woods a few miles."

"Okay." Bree tipped her head and watched him. She listened close as he explained when and where to look for his turn off.

He handed her the paper. "My cell is listed there, too."

"Looks easy enough. Thanks." Bree reached across and took the pen, then scribbled a number down and ripped it off. "Here's my number, just in case something comes up between now and then."

Darren pocketed the note and stood with plate in hand. "Stel, I'm going to take off."

"Thanks for fixing my faucet." Stella took the plate from him. "And you don't need to clean up, I got it."

"Thanks for dinner." Then he faced Bree. "See you Friday."

"Friday. I'll meet you at your place by eight-fifteen." She sounded so professional, like they'd scheduled a business meeting. Not a date.

"Sounds good." Ignoring the twist in his gut, Darren justified showing Bree around as an extension of his job.

A good word from Bree or her mom into the right ears might go a long way in upping his chances for the supervisor position. He'd take all the help he could to make sure he got the job this time.

He'd simply showcase the great up north outdoors and be done with it. When Bree left, he'd be done with her, too.

Chapter Four

By Friday night, the weather had turned chilly, so Bree dressed in warm layers. Who knew how long they'd be outside? Her parents thought she was crazy to venture out so late. Maybe they were right.

Following the map Darren had drawn was easy. She'd driven on the one main road heading north most of the way. Slowing down, she spotted the Honey for Sale sign right where he'd said it would be. Bree took the next right onto a dirt road. So far, so good.

Scanning the map again, she went another two miles until she saw the fish mailbox. This was Darren's driveway. It was a dirt two-track path similar to the ones they'd taken to find mushrooms. She slowed to a stop and stared at that mailbox.

What was she doing coming here?

With a deep breath, she squared her shoulders

and pulled into the two-mile drive. No regrets. No missed opportunities.

Her cell phone buzzed with an incoming text. She slowed to a stop and grabbed it, hoping it wasn't Darren changing their plans. Another text from Philip that she ignored.

Darren hadn't been kidding when he said he lived in the woods. She'd watched the sun dip low in the sky as she drove here, but the surrounding trees with new leaves blocked the dwindling light.

When she finally pulled into a large clearing, the wood home surprised her. She'd expected something far less airy than the chalet-style structure in front of her. Darren's home was small but pretty with a wraparound deck that was partly covered and sat atop a two-bay garage. Another metal garage stood nearby.

She smiled when she saw him outside with two small beagles. Both were brown and white with black backs, floppy ears and sweet faces. Darren hunched down to give them each a pat and scratch behind their ears. Tails wagging, they followed him around a fenced area begging for attention. He gave in and petted them some more.

Stella had assured her that Darren was a good guy, but the gentle way he treated his dogs proved it.

She parked her car, got out and looked around.

Wood stacked neatly under an overhang between the garage and stairway caught her eye. An axe lay against a beam with more wood scattered on the ground. She'd been spot-on with her lumberjack comparison. He even wore a padded flannel shirt.

"Hey." He gave her a cautious smile. "You're early."

Only fifteen minutes early. She walked toward the fenced dog run. "I gave myself extra time in case I got lost. Your dogs are adorable. What are their names?"

Darren stood facing her on the other side of the fence. "Mickey and Clara."

"Hi, guys." Bree stuck her fingers through the fence, and both dogs jostled to lick her hand in greeting. "Do they stay outside?"

"When I'm working. They have access to part of the garage so they can get out of the weather."

She nodded. "You have a nice home."

He looked surprised by her compliment. "Thanks. It's a prefab, but I've added a few things. The deck is one of them. I need to gather some gear, and then we can go. What size shoe do you wear?

"Seven and a half. Why?"

"I have a pair of waders that might fit you. Come in and try them on."

"Weighters?" Bree followed him through the open garage door into a spotless space without a single vehicle parked inside. The walls had shelves filled with all sorts of outdoor gear—fishing poles, snowshoes. She pointed to a big metal safe. "What's that?"

"Waders? They're pull-on overall boots to wade into the water."

"No, that big green thing in the corner."

"Gun cabinet."

She felt her eyes widen at the size of the thing. "You have a lot of guns."

He laughed. "I have firearms for both work and recreation. So, yeah. I have a few."

Her stomach tightened. She didn't know men with guns. Philip's anger over her residency had unsettled her big-time. It was the reason she finally broke it off with him. What would a big guy like Darren turn into when he was mad? Stella's assurance that he was safe shriveled to nothing in the presence of that green cabinet.

She spotted a deer head mounted on the opposite wall and wrinkled her nose. "So, you hunt, too."

"Yup." His eyes challenged her to make something of it. "I like to fill my freezer."

"Oh." Of course, he killed his own food. Who was she to raise an eyebrow? She ate meat with no thought to where it came from. Just like the morels.

"Have you ever tried venison?" His voice sounded softer now. More coaxing.

"No." She heard the whine of the dogs. They were inside the other garage bay that had been fenced off and poked their noses through the wire.

"It's good."

"Hmm. Maybe." She wrinkled her nose.

Darren laughed. "There are no maybes about it."

Bree ambled over to the dogs and gave them each a pat over the low fence, noticing their inside space looked pretty comfy. They had their own couch, water bowls and a basket of chew toys. This man took good care of his pets.

"Here, try these on. You'll stay warmer in these." He held out a pair of tan overalls with boots. *Waders.*

"So, you go into the water to catch these things?"

"You can net from shore, but that's not nearly as fun."

Bree was here to have fun, no matter how cold the thought of getting into a river at the end of April. She took the waders, found a chair to sit on and slipped off her sneakers. She'd never expected to do this sort of thing, so she hadn't brought any kind of boots with her up north. They'd already been shipped out to Seattle. Not that she owned a pair of real hiking boots. Maybe she'd buy a pair. She had a feeling trekking off the beaten path with Darren might be rough in spots.

She shoved one foot in, then the other, and stood.

"Walk a little. How do they feel?"

She galumphed her way around. "Big."

"I've got heavy socks upstairs. Come on."

She slipped out of the waders and followed him in her stocking feet, leaving her sneakers on the floor. She wanted a peek at the inside of his house. That said a lot about a man, didn't it? Too bad she hadn't paid attention to Philip's showy high-rise apartment.

Stepping onto the main floor, she was far from enlightened other than another deer head mounted over the fireplace and some fish on another wall. Darren's house had an open floor plan with a living room, a dining area and a kitchen with stainless steel appliances. Pretty but plain in neutral shades. The opposite wall was floor-to-ceiling windows.

Stepping closer to the windows, she peered outside. Woods surrounded most of Darren's property, but there was an open field to the left that went on for days. Rolling hills beyond completed the idyllic view.

"I'll be right back." Darren disappeared down a short hallway into what must have been his bedroom.

Bree barely heard him. She walked around,

touching the stone fireplace and scoping out the upstairs loft with a wrought iron railing facing those windows. What a perfect spot to practice her cello with such an inspiring view. Too bad the music room at Bay Willows faced the little post office instead of the lake.

"Here, that should do it, and your feet will stay warm."

She took the thick woolen socks from him. "Thank you. You have a beautiful view."

He narrowed his gaze as if questioning her sincerity. "I think so."

Maybe his ex-fiancée hadn't thought so. Maybe the plain walls other than dead animals didn't appeal. The waders Bree had tried on had to have been Raleigh's. They were too small for Darren. Somehow Bree couldn't picture Stella's tall, model-like granddaughter trussed up in rubber waders. Bree couldn't imagine her here, either, amid the multiple shades of tan and lack of artwork. The lack of flair.

He gave her an odd look as if considering her for something. "Follow me."

Bree's stomach flipped. "Where?"

But he was already in the kitchen, opening the fridge and pulling out a pot.

"What's that?"

He lifted the lid and plunged a fork inside. "Venison stew. Wanna try it?"

Bree wrinkled her nose. "Cold?"

He chuckled. "Not quite. I had it for dinner tonight."

She hesitated, not sure she wanted to venture quite that far, but then squared her shoulders. This outing was about trying new things. She stepped forward, waders and socks in hand.

Darren held the fork for her, cupping his hand underneath. "Go ahead."

She stalled, looking into his eyes. "You made this?"

He laughed. A low, soft rumble that sounded incredibly masculine. "Don't worry. I can cook."

Bree took in the forkful offered and chewed. The venison was still warm and surprisingly tasty. She glanced at Darren again.

He watched her closely. "Well?"

"Good." Her voice came out sounding strangely hoarse.

It was then that Bree saw her attraction reflected back from Darren's blue eyes. He had to feel it, too—this strange stirring of the senses. For a moment, the only thing she heard was the increased beat of her pulse pounding like crazy.

He stepped back and set the fork in the sink with a clatter. "Ready?"

Bree nodded. "As ready as I'll ever be, I suppose."

Darren chuckled as he returned the pot to the fridge. "Let's go."

She blew out her breath and followed him back downstairs. Slipping into her sneakers and then clutching the heavy woolen socks and waders close, she climbed into Darren's white pickup truck. What had just happened?

"I can put those in the back," Darren offered as he clicked on the radio and country music whispered.

"I'm good." Bree spied the slim backseat and clutched the socks and waders closer as if they'd protect her from the odd sensations flooding her.

Darren turned up the volume to an upbeat song that crooned about the mysteries between a man and a woman. Hearing some guy sing about kissing in the morning didn't help. Not at all. Bree tapped her toe on the floor in time with the beat, hoping to dispel whatever it was that Darren had done to her with merely a smile.

She'd never met anyone like Darren before. Having grown up downstate, Bree hadn't been exposed to things like venison, guns or smelt dipping. Was she ready for what lay ahead?

A shiver raced through her despite the warmth of the truck's heater. Tonight promised something she craved. Not only a break from her usual routine but also adventurous freedom before she made one of the biggest time commitments of her life.

She'd wanted a change, and tonight definitely ranked as different. Only, she hoped this inconvenient attraction to Darren would pass. She'd worked with nice-looking musicians without any trouble. Maybe this was merely a temporary curiosity because Darren wasn't like the urbane men she was used to. He was different. A passing fancy that would eventually vanish. Once her vacation was over.

Darren parked his truck next to his friend's SUV and got out. The pungently sweet smell of burning wood hung in the air. There were several other vehicles parked in the small clearing off a two-track path. The place was crowded.

He looked up at the clear sky tinted pink with the memory of this evening's sunset. A big crescent moon hung just above the tree line. It wouldn't shed much light later—not quite the blue moonlight he'd promised—but then, he had flashlights.

"Something wrong?" Bree climbed out of his truck.

"Our moon is nothing but a weak sliver tonight."

She looked up. "Still very pretty."

Like her.

He slipped into his waders. "You'd better put yours on. The grass looks wet." He handed her a pair of the smallest work gloves he had. "Here. Those thin knit gloves you're wearing won't keep you warm. You can slip these on top as protection against the cold when dipping nets."

"Thanks." Bree settled back in the passenger seat and slipped off her sneakers. She made quick work of getting into the wool socks and waders that were too long for her. She stuffed her cell phone and the gloves he gave her into the front pocket, shut the truck's door and joined him. "Ready."

Darren nodded, scanning her from head to toe. "Are you warm enough? I have an extra sweatshirt in the truck."

"I'm good." She wore a dark brown knit hat that matched her hair. Hair that had been gathered into a long, fat braid.

"Here, follow me." He handed her a stack of buckets while he carried their nets and a couple of flashlights, and they made their way toward the river.

Lantern lights and bonfires shone from various spots along the wooded shoreline. Dark water with glimmers of reflected light gurgled as it flowed. He heard raucous laughter but nothing worse. He might be off duty, but if anyone got out of hand, he'd take a look. They weren't the only ones out here hoping to enjoy the evening. He'd do what he could to make sure it stayed enjoyable—for everyone.

"Hey." His friend Neil gave them a wave.

Kate, Neil's wife, openly gaped, surprised to

see him with a woman. Especially a woman like Bree. "'Bout time."

Darren ignored the double meaning. Kate had been after him to date someone, anyone, as long as he quit dwelling on his ex. He quickly made the introductions. "Any smelt?"

"We've caught a few." Neil tipped his bucket to reveal a small pile of little silver fish.

He glanced at Bree, standing by the fire with her bare hands stretched toward the heat. The waders he'd purchased as a gift for Raleigh were too big for her. They bunched around Bree's knees and ankles, making her look like a girl playing dress-up in adult clothes. "Ready to give it a try?"

She walked toward him, nearly tripping. "That's what I'm here for."

He should have noticed how long the waders were before they'd left the house. But then, her presence had knocked him a bit off kilter. Darren fished around in the front pocket of his waders and found what he'd wanted.

He held up a decent length of thin rope. "Come here."

She looked at it, eyes wide and wary. "What for?"

He pulled the rope taut and laughed. "I'm not going to tie you up. It's a belt. Pull those waders up as high as you can."

"Oh." The relief in her voice made him smile

as she stepped forward. "You know, it's not very nice to brandish a rope like that."

"I'll remember that." He looped the rope around her waist and brought her close. Much too close. He inhaled that soft, flowery scent she wore and tied the rope with an awkward jerk that nearly landed her against his chest. He glanced at her face. Those plump lips of hers tempted, but what knocked him for a loop were her golden eyes wide with wonder.

She studied him.

He focused on her shoulder straps. "Better?"

"Much better. Thank you." Her voice sounded breathless.

Darren quickly stepped back before he did something stupid. He looked around to get his bearings and spotted Neil and Kate with their nets ready. They watched him and Bree instead of heading into the river.

Neil gave him a *thattaboy* nod.

Darren shook his head. Even though he found Bree attractive, he wasn't going to act on his feelings. No way. "Ready to wade in?"

"I am."

"Okay, watch your step. The rocks are slippery. We don't have to go very far. The smelt pool close to shore." He flashed the light. "See, there are a few right there."

Bree gripped his arm tightly and leaned over for a peek. "Look at that."

"You can stay on shore and dip if you want."

She shook her head. "Nope, I'm going in, but can I hold on to you?"

Those simple words pierced, reminding him that Raleigh hadn't wanted to hold on. She'd cut him loose to swim in a faster stream. He couldn't let Bree get under his skin. She was leaving; Maple Springs wasn't enough to keep her happy. He wouldn't be enough to keep her happy either.

"Yeah, sure." Darren put some distance between them to arrange their buckets along the shoreline. He handed her a net and then offered his hand.

She slipped on the gloves he'd given her. They were too big. He held tight while her eyes darted nervously along the river's edge. "You won't let go?"

"Not till you say it's okay."

She slowly followed him into the river.

The dark water was high from the winter snow melt and the current a little stronger than normal, but certainly not fast and not deep. Not where they stood up to their knees. Something about the way Bree trusted him to keep her safe made him want to do just that. "I'm going to pull you to me so you can dip your net in, okay?"

She nodded.

He wrapped his arm around her trim waist and shone the flashlight on the water, giving up flashes of silver from beneath the surface. "Go ahead and dip your net in. I got you."

Bree dipped her net with one hand while holding on to his waders with the other. She wasn't taking any chances. She pulled up a few smelt and laughed at the squirming little fish.

"It's as easy as that," he said.

She looked up at him smiling. Her golden eyes looked darker at night, and the creases of her dimples faded with her smile. "Now what?"

His gaze strayed to her mouth. He wouldn't mind smearing that lipstick. "We put them in the buckets."

She let go of him. "I think I can do this."

He loosened his hold. "I know you can."

It wasn't that hard to stay upright, but then, Bree had never done this before. He watched her make her way back to shore, where she emptied her net. Then she carefully trudged back to him, refusing his offer of a steady hand.

Neil and Kate were in the water ahead of them.

"So, what do you do with all of these smelt?"

"We clean and then fry them."

"Are they good?" She looked doubtful.

"You'll have to find out for yourself." A fish fry meant another outing with Bree, unless she declined. But seeing the rapt expression on her face, he realized that wasn't going to happen. She clearly enjoyed this.

"But they're so small."

"You liked the venison, right?"

"Right." Bree dipped her net again, bringing in a few more. "Hey, look at that load."

They dipped and dumped until they'd nearly filled a gallon bucket. Bree's teeth chattered, but she hadn't complained. Not once.

"Ready for a break? We can warm up by the fire."

"Yess-ss."

He held out his hand to help her back to shore. She took it, letting go as soon as they were safe and sound on the river's bank. Kate and Neil were already seated around the fire, roasting hot dogs on sticks.

"Want one?" Kate offered him the package. "Bree, there's also pop and water in the cooler."

"Thank you." Bree stood close to the fire. Her phone buzzed, and she pulled it out from deep within the waders. Her mouth formed a grim line when she looked at it.

"Everything okay?" He grabbed a stick, skewered a dog onto it and then offered it to Bree before fixing a double for himself.

"It's nothing." She slipped her phone back where it came from and held her stick over the flames. "How often do you guys do this?"

"Once a year. Maybe twice, but it's a short spawning run. There are not nearly as many smelt as when my dad brought me here years ago," Kate said. "And with the DNR's limit of only two gallons per person…"

Darren laughed. "I don't write the rules. I enforce them."

"But not tonight." Neil poked his stick downriver at the other smelt dippers.

Darren shrugged. "Not unless I see something troubling."

Bree's eyes widened, but she didn't say anything.

He didn't look for trouble, but if he saw it, he'd do something about it. It was what he did. It was who he was.

Bree turned to Kate. "So, you grew up here?"

"I did, yes. What about you? Just here for the summer?" How'd Kate guess that? But then, one look at Bree confirmed she wasn't a local. If the red lipstick wasn't a dead giveaway, it was everything else about her. The way she moved, dressed, even talked with that slight lilt in her voice.

"My family owns a summer cottage in Bay Willows. I'm staying for a few weeks before moving out west." Bree rolled her hot dog and watched it sizzle.

Kate flashed him a look of concern.

Yeah, okay, maybe he was a glutton for punishment.

"How'd you two meet?" Kate asked.

"My mom organized a wild edibles class and Darren is our facilitator." Bree reached for a bun.

"Oh, nice." Kate handed over the mustard.

With his hot dogs roasted to perfection and nestled inside buns, Darren offered Bree a seat on an overturned bucket by the fire. It didn't take him long to wolf down his first dog. He glanced at Bree. She squeezed a dainty line of mustard along the center of her hot dog and ate with precise, ladylike bites.

"Back in the pond, I see." Neil stood next to him.

Darren splattered mustard on his second hot dog and took a bite. "Not even testing the waters."

"Right." Neil laughed at him.

Before Darren could protest, he spotted a beam of light that bobbed along the path they'd come down. A fellow conservation officer stepped through the brush, checking smelt limits. Stan nodded toward him. "Hey, Darren. How'd you guys do?"

"Just a couple of buckets. Not much, but enough."

"No trouble this evening?"

"Tame crowd," Darren answered.

"Good. I'm hoping for an early night." Stan hesitated. "When will you hear about Teri's spot?"

"I don't know. Soon." Darren finished his second hot dog.

"We're pulling for you."

"Thanks," Darren said.

Stan gave them a wave. "Good night."

"So, you're going for the area supervisor position again?" Neil asked.

Darren nodded. "Yep."

"It'll steep you pretty deep in town. You sure you want that?"

Like he needed a warning. "I know."

"Wait, what's wrong with in town?" Bree asked.

"The summer crowd drives him nuts."

"Oh? And why's that?" Bree cocked her head in challenge. She looked about as tough as an angry kitten.

Darren shrugged. "I don't like crowds."

"Not to mention he hasn't set foot in downtown Maple Springs in over a year and a half." Neil gave him a teasing shove. "That right?"

"Pretty much sums it up." Darren stretched. He wasn't getting into any of his reasons why. Not here, not with Bree. "I'm going to dip some more."

Bree stood. "I'll go, too. I want to get that limit."

"You going to clean them?" Amazed that she was into this, Darren had thrown down the challenge.

She picked it right up. "If you show me how."

"Tomorrow night, my house. We'll clean and fix what we catch here." He gestured toward Kate and Neil. "I'll invite them, too."

"Deal." Bree waded in next to him without any assistance.

She dipped like a pro. Not that it was hard, but he hadn't expected her to take to it so quickly. Raleigh would never have done this. She wouldn't have tried venison, either. Bree had nerve. He'd give her that.

The night wore on, and when they finally packed up to head for home, Darren noticed Bree huddled in the passenger seat, looking frozen. "It'll take a minute or two before the heat kicks in."

Bree considered him. "Is it true that you haven't been in town for almost two years?"

"I go to church, and that's downtown." Instead of expanding, Darren joked, "It's better not to listen to what Neil says."

Bree kept digging. "Is it because of Stella's granddaughter?"

"Something like that." He didn't want to come face-to-face with her and Tony and react. He didn't want to talk about it, either.

"Oh." Bree's brow furrowed, but she got the message and let it drop.

He drove the rest of the way home in silence. It wasn't far, but Bree had put her head back and closed her eyes. Surely she hadn't fallen asleep that fast, but then, it was after one in the morning when he turned into his driveway.

Bree sat up straight and looked around, getting her bearings. She *had* fallen asleep.

Nice. He put women to sleep. That was about right. Boring local yokel. Nothing exciting here. He cleared his throat. "Be careful driving back to town."

She looked confused at his sharp tone. "Don't you want help unloading the smelt?"

"No. I got it." He was confused by his sudden irritation, too. He suddenly didn't like the idea of her driving alone in the wee hours, but unless he followed her home, there wasn't much else he could do. He couldn't offer that she stay here. "Keep an eye out for deer and drive slow."

She narrowed her gaze, looking offended, as if he'd told her she couldn't take care of herself. "Would you like me to text you when I get home?"

Her sarcasm wasn't lost on him. "Yeah, do that. I'm serious. Deer move at night."

"Okay, okay. See you tomorrow." She slid behind the wheel of her small Subaru and rolled down the window as if she'd forgotten something. "Thanks, Darren, for taking me smelt dipping."

Surprised at her sincerity, he gave her a nod. "You're welcome."

He unloaded the truck as she backed out. Placing the smelt in the extra refrigerator he had in the garage, he couldn't believe he looked forward

to tomorrow night. Would Bree surprise him yet
again by cleaning their catch?

Twenty minutes later, he got his answer when
his phone whistled with Bree's incoming text.

Made it home fine. Thanks again for tonight. I had
a great time off the beaten path.

He smiled and texted back, It was fun. He
meant it.

Really fun! Looking forward to cleaning 2morrow.
Good night.

Good night.

He slipped his phone in his pocket.

Bree might be cut from the same cloth as
Raleigh, but her pattern was completely different. Bree had treated Kate and Neil with warm
respect, and they'd jumped on the fish fry invi-
tation. They liked her.

He did, too.

Maybe all Bree wanted was to have fun, plain
and simple. Nothing complicated. There was no
reason they couldn't keep things that way. Maybe
if he showed Bree a good time, he'd learn to
have fun again, too. He needed that more than
he cared to admit. It didn't mean anything had
to change. He wouldn't have to change.

He could be friends with a woman without having to date her. Without needing to kiss her. Even Bree. Most especially Bree.

Chapter Five

"I'm heading out." Bree slipped on a cotton cardigan sweater over her T-shirt.

The warm day had dissolved into a chilly evening. Tonight she'd head to Darren's for their smelt dinner, and she'd pick up something at the store on her way to take. Maybe he'd build a fire in that huge fireplace of his and they could hang out and watch the flames dance.

Or maybe not. Really, where'd that idea come from?

"Philip called while you were out walking," her mother said.

Bree's good mood took a nosedive. She'd had her cell phone with her the whole time. Odd. Why didn't he call or text her? "What did he want?"

"He wanted to make sure you were okay."

Bree narrowed her gaze. "I'm fine."

"Maybe he's reconsidering."

"Reconsidering what?" *Being an idiot?* Bree didn't voice that thought.

"Breaking up. We had a long chat, and he's concerned for you."

"Concerned?" Bree should have set the record straight, but what was the point? If Philip wanted to think he'd ended it, fine. As long as he truly ended it and left her alone.

"What if you regret this decision? Seattle is a big move, and two years is a long time."

Bree gritted her teeth. She didn't need Philip stirring up more doubt in her parents' heads. The music residency couldn't have come at a better time. If she didn't spread her wings a little, she'd never know if she could fly. "This is the opportunity of a lifetime."

Her mother didn't look convinced. "But men like Philip don't grow on trees."

At twenty-nine, Bree was old enough to make her own decisions, but her parents still wanted her tucked into a prestigious marriage like the one her sister had. She grabbed her purse. "He's not for me."

"Surely you're not enamored with this DNR fella you're going to see."

"No, Mom, I'm not." She'd explained that Darren's friends would be there, too. This wasn't a date or anything. Besides, *attracted* wasn't even close to *enamored*. She'd be safe. "For the next twenty-four months, I won't have time for any *fella*."

Bree meant that, even though her heart skipped at the thought of Darren near that fireplace. "I've got to go."

"Oh, one more thing. Jan Nelson called. She wondered if you'd play next weekend for the Mother's Day brunch at the Maple Springs Inn. They need a cello."

"Sure, I'll call her." Jan was a board member of the Bay Willows Association and the driving force behind starting a summer music school. It was probably going to be some kind of music camp for kids, but Bree wouldn't mind finding out if there were future plans for anything more intensive.

"And Philip?"

Bree let out a sigh. "I'll let him know I'm fine."

Her mother smiled. "Thank you and be careful."

"I will." Careful might as well have been her middle name.

As a teen, Bree had never roughhoused or played sports like her sister for fear of any injury keeping her away from the cello. As a college student, she'd buried herself with a double major in performing arts and music composition. Then there'd been overseas opportunities and getting her master's while making her way up within the strings section of the symphony orchestra. Where was the fun, frivolous stuff?

Tonight she'd clean fish with Darren and his friends. *She'd clean fish!* That's something she'd never done before. She might not like it once she saw what it entailed, but Bree wanted no regrets and no missed opportunities. She needed to do fun stuff before focusing every ounce of her energy on music once again.

Could she compete at the level she was about to step up to? She had to. Bree wanted more than playing someone else's music all the time. She'd create her own, have it heard and somehow make an impact.

With God's grace, she'd figure it all out. But she had to be proactive. That meant cleaning the small silvery fish she'd helped catch the night before while standing in a freezing-cold river with a burly man she barely knew. That kind of gumption was what she needed to practice more of if she wanted to succeed.

"So, what's with you and Bree?" Kate cornered Darren in the kitchen.

He shrugged. "She wants to experience new things, and I offered to show her the area."

Kate looked skeptical. "Uh-huh."

"Hey, you're the one who said I should start dating."

That made his friend's wife look even more concerned. "I meant someone local, not someone who's moving away in a month. A lot can happen in a month."

He knew all about that. "Nothing will happen at all. We're just having some fun."

"Leave him alone, Kate." Neil carried in a bucket of the smelt and set it on the table, followed by Darren's brother Cam.

"Who's Bree?" Cam asked.

Darren clenched his teeth before he snarled at all of them. "No one. Look, it's no big deal. She's not looking to get involved and neither am I. Besides, she's not my type."

"She's exactly your type," Neil said with a laugh.

Darren looked at him sharply. "What's that supposed to mean?"

"She's different, and you like different."

Cam laughed. "He's got a point."

That much was probably true. Darren had dated his share, not finding anyone he'd wanted to settle down with until Raleigh had knocked him for a loop. His ex-fiancée had been nothing like the girls he'd gone out with before. Nothing like his sisters either, who'd grown up knowing how to take care of themselves out-of-doors.

"No one from Bay Willows is my type," Darren grumbled. He'd been there, done that. And he wouldn't do it again. Not if he was smart.

A knock at the door scattered his thoughts. Glancing toward the storm door, he saw Bree standing on the other side, and his pulse picked up speed. Was she truly different? Probably not. She might look different, but where she came from made her the same as everything he didn't want.

He opened the door. "Hey."

Bree looked around. "Where are your dogs?"

"Downstairs until after we eat."

She lifted a brown paper bag. "I brought a few things for dinner."

"Great." He peeked inside at a container of coleslaw next to chocolate bars, marshmallows and graham crackers. "S'mores?"

"I thought maybe later by the fire—" She looked a little flustered. "They make good dessert."

"Yeah, sure." He backed away to let her pass. Her hair had been twisted into a knot at the back of her head, and she wore a soft yellow sweater and jeans. She looked great. Much too nice to scoop the guts out of smelt.

"You sure you want to do this?"

She stopped walking and looked up at him, wrinkling her nose. "Is it really bad?"

He chuckled. "No. It's just…"

Her gaze narrowed. "What?"

He glanced at her shoulders. "That looks like a good sweater."

"No worries. I've got a T-shirt underneath." She turned and headed for the kitchen.

Darren scratched his head and followed her. She might change her tune once they got the assembly line set up. But then, something about the determined line of those narrow shoulders told him she was on a mission.

He wasn't sure what that was all about, but hearing her give Kate and Neil a warm greeting did something to him. Something scary. He got the crazy impression that his house felt more like a home with her in it.

"And this is my brother Cam. He's staying for dinner, too." Darren was glad for that. It made the night less like a double date.

Bree held out her hand. "Nice to meet you."

"Likewise." Cam gave her a wink.

Bree quickly pulled away and headed for the fireplace. Her eyes glowed. "You built a fire!"

"To take the chill off." Darren didn't know what else to say. She looked so pleased, and he wished his friends and brother were anywhere else but here.

"See, those s'mores will come in handy." Her dimples showed.

He'd never roasted marshmallows inside before, but doing that with Bree seemed dangerous somehow. "Huh."

She slipped off her sweater, revealing a white top that was far from his idea of a simple T-shirt with its ruffled hem. "So, what do we do now?"

Neil gave Cam a pointed look. "Maybe we should disappear."

Cam laughed and headed for the recliner. "I'm watching the news."

Darren quit gawking. He was thinking too much about making those s'mores. "We'll set up an assembly line to clean, dredge and then fry up the smelt."

Bree padded straight to his sink and washed her hands. "I'm ready."

Kate laughed. "You might want to work at my end with the flour and frying."

Bree shook her head. "No way. I caught them. I need to learn how to clean them."

Kate raised her eyebrows and glanced at him.

Darren shrugged. One thing he'd learned about Bree—she went at a task with determination. He'd never seen anyone work this hard to *have fun*. "Let me show you what to do, and then you can decide."

He grabbed the half-full bucket of smelt and set it next to the sink, then washed up. Taking one of the small fish in one hand and scissors in the other, he turned to Bree. "First, we make a cut at the back of the head, and then another cut along the underside starting from the tail, like so, up toward the head."

Bree watched closely. "Then what?"

"Then gently pull the head away and all the innards come with it. See?" He showed her the cleaned out smelt. It wasn't a messy process. Cleaning smelt was easier than filleting other fish. It simply took longer because there were more of them. "We rinse them real good, bread them and fry them."

"Okay." She sounded a little shaky.

He laughed. "You don't have to do this."

Bree stared at the smelt. "Yes, I do."

"Why? What's with all this trying new things?"

She squared her shoulders. "It's a confidence booster."

This woman seemed confident to him. Her choppy bangs screamed that she didn't care what people thought, but maybe it was all a ruse. A front to hide behind, like Raleigh had hidden behind that rebellious spirit of hers.

He wanted to know why Bree needed a confidence boost, but he didn't ask. The less he knew about her down deep, the better. "Want to cut or clean?"

Looking like she approached a dissection assignment in science class, Bree considered the options, then finally answered, "I don't think I can use scissors like that, so I'll do the cleaning."

"Alright, let's get started." He glanced at Neil, who'd finished making the flour coating. "We'll get a few cleaned in advance."

His buddy grabbed a couple of beverages from the fridge and joined his wife and Cam in the living room to catch the local news. "Take your time."

Darren looked at Bree. "Ready?"

"Yes."

He made the cut and handed the fish over.

She tried to grab the head, hesitated and then tried again.

"Like this." Darren covered her hand with his own. "Stick your index finger in where I made the cut here and then pull down."

She looked up at him, her eyes wide and inviting.

Darren didn't look away. "See, not bad."

"No. Not bad at all." Her voice sounded soft and a little breathless.

Awareness kicked him hard. He wasn't so sure they were talking about the fish. He quickly let go of her hand, concentrated on the next smelt and handed it over. "Here, try on your own."

Bree did as asked, without hesitation this time. Then she rinsed the fish off and tossed it in the big stainless steel bowl he'd placed on the counter next to her.

"Good job."

"Thanks." She reached for the next one.

Darren obliged with one smelt after the other. Soon Bree was cleaning them like a pro, but she refused to cut the heads. They kicked up the pace when Kate joined them to heat up the oil in a big fry pan.

They'd soon have dinner, and then what? Roasting marshmallows by the fire sure sounded like something to do on a date. He hoped Neil and Kate didn't leave early. Cam would no doubt duck out after dinner.

All Darren knew was that he didn't want to be left alone with Bree.

Bree took a deep breath when dinner was finally on the table. She needed to sit as far away from Darren as possible. It was bad enough standing close by the sink where their fingers touched every time he handed her a smelt.

Maybe she'd imagined the mushroom cloud of awareness that had billowed between them. Maybe it was all one-sided. Hers. Explosive attraction was foreign to her. She'd never felt this way with Philip. Was never drawn to him the way Darren pulled at her with invisible strings.

"Let's pray so we can eat." Kate sat down and reached for her husband's hand on one side and Cam's on the other.

Oh, no. Not more hand-holding. Bree slipped into the only open chair across from Kate, putting her right next Darren. Okay, maybe sitting next to him, she wouldn't get lost in his bright blue eyes.

"Neil, do you mind?" He wrapped his hand around hers. Darren had honest hands, callused in spots and work-worn. Warm and strong.

Bree bowed her head and listened to the prayer of gratitude for the food. Surprised when Neil mentioned her name, she looked up.

"Guide her, Lord, in this next step of her life. Amen."

Darren surprised her even more by squeezing her hand before letting go. No one had ever prayed so specifically for her before. She looked at Neil. "Thank you."

Neil smiled. "You're welcome."

"So, what's up?" Cam asked.

"I'm moving to Seattle for a music residency there." Bree accepted the platter of fried smelt and stared at it. She'd caught them, cleaned them, and now it was time to eat them. Could she do it?

"Don't worry about the bones," Cam said. "You can't tell they're even there."

Bree nodded and scooped a few onto her plate.

"How long will you be gone?" Cam asked.

"Two years." Bree looked around the table, watching the others fill their plates. She took a tentative bite of fish. It was good. Really good. So when the platter was set before her, she grabbed a few more.

"Will you stay out there afterward, then? At the end you'll have a job waiting for you?" Kate offered her the bowl of coleslaw.

"Maybe." A lot depended on her. Was she good enough actually to compose? She wouldn't ever give up her cello, but it'd be nice to do more, maybe even mentor others. There were tons of opportunities out west where the music business spanned so much wider for composition than here, in the Midwest.

"We may never see you again," Kate said.

Bree knew this had been stated for Darren's benefit. His friends were trying to protect him. From her. It was laughable considering how timid she'd been dating Philip. Until recently, she'd never rocked the boat. It wouldn't be smart to get involved with someone whose roots were planted so deep here. "I suppose that might be true."

"Her parents have a place in Bay Willows." Darren winked at her.

Bree smiled. "I guess I'll be back sometime. I can't imagine a better place for summer vacations."

"I can. It's called the Bahamas," Neil said.

They all laughed.

Bree turned to Darren. "Where do you go on vacation?"

Darren shrugged. "The Upper Peninsula, mostly. My uncle has a camp there."

Bree tipped her head. "Like a whole campground?"

He chuckled. "No, it's a cabin on a small lake."

"I've never been to the UP."

He looked at her, shocked. "Never been over the bridge?"

She shrugged. There had never been a reason to go. "Nope."

"Something you should remedy before you leave." Cam scooped more smelt onto his plate.

"Oh, I've seen it. I've been to Mackinac Island." Bree knew the beauty of the five-mile-long Mighty Mac. She'd even toured the bridge museum in Mackinaw City.

"Take her for a burger at that drive-in restaurant," Neil said.

Darren chuckled. "Yeah, maybe."

Bree didn't jump on that one. It sounded too much like a real date, and she wasn't looking to *date* Darren. Getting to know him better was fine, as long as it remained friendly. "I think I'd rather see those elk roaming."

Darren nodded. "We can do that."

Cam looked aghast, as if they were both crazy. "Yeah, there's a real good time."

Bree glanced between brothers. The resemblance was strong, but Cam was blond and struck her as a flirt.

Finished with dinner, Bree helped Kate clear the table while the guys took the makings for s'mores into the living room.

Bree handed Kate the platter with a few left-over smelt.

"Thanks." Kate hesitated as if grappling with something she wanted to say.

"What?" Bree prodded.

Kate waved her hand in dismissal. "Nothing."

Bree knew it was something and more than likely something about Darren. And her. "I know you're concerned for him because of his broken engagement and all."

Kate's eyes grew wide. "He told you about that?"

"Stella, Raleigh's grandmother, is a friend of mine. She told me her granddaughter broke it off."

"Did she tell you how?" Kate glanced into the living room to be sure they weren't overheard. The guys had the TV tuned into a baseball game. The volume was up and they were loud too.

Bree had never been very good at listening or remembering rumors, but the look on Kate's face clued her in that this wasn't going to be good. "No. Not really."

"He won't talk about it." Kate lowered her voice to a mere whisper. "But his bride ran off with the best man the night before the wedding."

Bree's stomach dropped. "Wow…"

"Yeah. 'Wow.' He's had a rough time of it." Kate loaded up the dishwasher with the plates Bree had stacked on the counter.

"It's no wonder." And no wonder he was wary. Bree couldn't imagine the sting of that kind of betrayal.

Kate stopped arranging dishes and looked at

Bree. "He fell pretty hard and got engaged only a month after meeting her."

Bree's mind whirled. She gripped the counter as if it were the room spinning and not her thoughts. Her heart. Darren didn't dawdle when it came to falling in love.

"You two coming in or what?" Darren poked his head around the corner.

Bree glanced at Kate. Had he heard them?

"We're on our way." Kate gave her a pointed look, then whispered, "He'd have a fit if he knew I'd told you."

Bree made a zipping gesture across her lips. Walking into the living room, Bree drew close to the hearth and sat down on the floor. The snap and crackle of the fire soothed, but she couldn't get what Kate said out of her head. Only a month. He'd decided to spend the rest of his life with someone after only a month.

Would Darren truly be mad if he knew that she knew?

"Here." Darren handed her one of a handful of metal skewers with a couple marshmallows stuck on the end.

"Thanks." She held it over the flames, watching the white puff of sugar slowly turn brown. The mellow warmth of burning wood coupled with a hearty dinner made Bree's eyelids droop.

"Tired?" Darren sat next to her.

Maybe she was too comfortable here, hanging

out with Darren's friends and even his brother. And maybe she wanted to know more than she should about this man who once gave his heart so easily. She raised her s'more. "After this, I'd better go."

"Thanks for coming."

"Are you kidding? It was great. I like smelt. The whole thing."

Darren laughed. "You did good cleaning them."

The compliment warmed her more than the fire. "Thanks."

"Here, your marshmallow's about to fall." Darren held out a graham cracker layered with chocolate.

Bree concentrated on getting the wobbly mass of mallow in between the crackers without dropping it and then laughed when she succeeded. "Aren't you having one?"

Darren shrugged. "Not much of a s'more guy."

"I love these things. In a pinch, I've made them over the gas stove in my apartment." Bree took a bite, smearing melted chocolate all over the corner of her mouth. A gooey bit of marshmallow stuck to her chin. She wiped it off with the heel of her hand. Her fingers were sticky, too.

"You have chocolate right here, in that crazy dimple." Darren wiped near her cheek.

Bree froze, hardly breathing.

"I do like chocolate." He licked his thumb. "And dimples."

She panicked at the softness of Darren's voice and glanced toward the couch. Kate and Neil snuggled at one end, glued to the ball game, and Darren's brother had gone into the kitchen and returned with a glass of water. She connected with his smirking gaze, and her stomach turned. Had he seen them?

Cam gave her a saucy wink.

She felt her cheeks flush with heat. That answered that. She needed to get out of here fast. Another two bites and her s'more was gone. Bree brushed her hands off on her jeans and stood. "I'm going to head home."

Darren stood, too. "I'll walk you to the door."

"Thanks."

"Good night, Bree." Kate gave her a wave, and her husband did the same.

"Be careful," Cam said and then chuckled.

Bree knew her face was on fire. The rest of her was, too. Really, this wasn't good. She heard the beagles bellow from downstairs and was grateful for the distraction. "Your dogs?"

"They want up."

"Aww, I didn't get to see them." Bree wasn't about to stay, though.

"Next time." Darren opened the door and leaned against the frame. "You okay to drive home?"

"I'll be fine." But she'd stifled a yawn. "I'll text you when I get there."

The dogs barked again.

Bree needed to leave. She opened the storm door, glad for the cool night air. "See you at class."

"Good night, Bree." His deep voice sounded dangerously sweet.

"Night." She scrambled off the deck and skipped down the steps as quickly as possible.

She'd had fun this evening. Maybe too much fun, and certainly too much food and too much of Darren. Near him, she got a heady feeling as if she'd drunk wine. Not good.

Slipping into the driver's seat, she started her car, and her phone buzzed from inside her purse. She'd left it in the car. Two messages from Philip. One a text, the other a voice mail with an agitated male voice asking where she was.

Pulling out of the driveway, she returned the call.

"Bree, 'bout time—"

She cut him off. "Philip, this has got to stop. Why do you keep calling me?"

"I want to make sure you're okay."

"I'm fine."

"Still accepting that residency?"

"I'm not backing out." Not for anything.

Silence.

"Philip, I've got to go. I'm driving. And please stop calling."

"Driving? Where are you?"

"That's none of your concern." Her voice sounded shrill.

"Fine." He sounded annoyed. Then his tone softened. "Okay. Take care, Bree."

Maybe this would be it. Maybe he'd finally gotten the message that they were through. "You, too."

The chill air made her shiver. Rolling up her window, she reached for her sweater and realized she'd left it at Darren's. She'd text him to bring it to class when she got home.

Home.

Here couldn't be home. There were no opportunities for her here. Right now, she didn't have a place to call home, and yet there was something about the way Darren made her feel at home with him. She thought about what Kate had told her. Darren had asked Raleigh to marry him after only a month. She'd never thought that possible before. Never thought feelings could be real after such a short time. But now—

She repeated what she'd told Philip out loud and with volume. "I'm not backing out of this residency. Not for anything or anyone."

Chapter Six

Sunday morning, Darren stepped out of the church he'd attended all his life. He still went where his parents went along with some of his siblings. He didn't see any reason to change. Attending his traditional church service was the one place he didn't worry about running into Tony or Raleigh.

His reluctance to try another church had been one of the many bones of contention he'd had with his ex-fiancée. He liked going where he'd gone since childhood, but Raleigh didn't. In hindsight, maybe he should have been more flexible, tried someplace else. It was too easy to go through the motions here, where he'd never had to get involved deeper than simply showing up.

"Brrr…" His mom pulled her jacket closer. "It's chilly today."

"Supposed to get even colder." His dad stood on the wide church steps and surveyed downtown.

"Not expected to warm up for a few days yet." Usually in a rush to leave, today Darren wasn't in a hurry to head for his empty home. He followed his father's gaze over Maple Springs. The leaves on the trees were still young with that spring-green crayon color. Main Street lay sleepy on this cold morning before the town swelled with summer residents and tourists.

"As long as it doesn't snow on Mother's Day, I'm good." His mom tucked her arm into the crook of Darren's elbow. "Come to breakfast with us. It's your favorite place."

Simply called Dean's Hometown Grille, the tiny restaurant was right around the corner and probably packed. He used to go there a lot with Tony. Darren swallowed hard. Maybe he wasn't feeling *that* brave.

"Hey, isn't that your girlfriend over there?" Cam had exited the church and pointed.

Darren spotted Bree walking toward them from across the street. "She's not my girlfriend."

His mom's eyes widened. "Why didn't you tell me you're seeing someone?"

"Darren's got a girlfriend? Will wonders never cease?" His sister Monica joined the gawkers. "Who is she?"

"Just a friend." There was no use correcting them. They wouldn't believe him, anyway.

Bree waved and crossed the street. Pretty in dark leggings and a long sweater, she headed straight for them with a smile that made those dimples flash. She wore the same brown knitted hat, and her hair was gathered into one long, fat braid.

His pulse kicked up a notch. *Great. Just great.*

When Bree stood at the base of the church steps, she smiled again. "Morning Darren, Cam."

"Meet my family. Some of them, anyway." Darren should have left when he'd had the chance.

"So, this is where you go to church. I go to the Bay Willows chapel." Before he could stop the inevitable, Bree extended a hand toward his mom. "Hi, I'm Bree Anderson."

"Helen Zelinsky." His mom eagerly returned the handshake. "And this is my husband, Andy. My daughter Monica, and you've met Cam."

"Last night at Darren's," Cam added.

His mom gave him that questioning look Darren knew to answer. "Bree is helping out with the wild edibles class at Bay Willows."

"Oh." His mom's eyes widened a bit more before focusing back on Bree. "How's he doing?"

"Wonderful. He really knows his stuff." Bree gave him a nod. "I saw Stella at services this morning, and we're looking forward to hunting for fiddleheads."

Darren nodded. "They can be elusive, but they're out there."

They fell into an awkward silence.

"Well, I'd better get back home." Bree dipped her head.

"We're headed for breakfast around the corner. Please, join us." His mom used her *don't-refuse-me* tone.

Darren could have kicked his mom, but letting Bree walk away would open up a can of questions he didn't feel like answering. He'd feel safer if she joined them. "You won't be sorry. The food's plain but good."

"Yeah?" Bree looked as if she weighed his words.

He meant it, and threw out a ready excuse. "Buying your breakfast is the least I can do considering your help with the class."

"Showing me the area is more than enough thanks."

His mom jumped on that like his beagles swarmed after hearing a scraped plate. "Are you moving here permanently?"

Bree laughed. "Oh, no. My parents have a summer cottage here—"

"I agreed to show her the nontouristy places before she leaves," Darren interrupted.

"I gotta run." Cam skipped down the steps. "Nice to see you again, Bree."

His mom didn't let it go. "What kind of places?"

"We went smelt dipping with Kate and Neil on Friday." This conversation was taking an odd turn, and Darren wanted it back on track.

"How'd you do?" His dad's eyes lit up. "I haven't been dipping in years."

"We got close to our limits." Darren scanned the streets. An old man walked his dog. Church-goers heading home. No one to worry about.

"I've never done anything like that before, and it was fun," Bree added.

"You poor thing." Monica laughed. "Darren's more at home outside than in. I've gotta run. Chamber meeting with Brady."

"On Sunday?" Darren knew it didn't matter the day. His sister had had a crush on the chamber of commerce president for a while now. The guy didn't know what he was in for. Or maybe he did, and that's why he'd never asked Monica out.

"As good a day as any other." Monica got all prickly as if daring him to make something of it.

He raised his hands in surrender. "Fine."

"Good," Monica sparred back.

His mom intervened. "Come on, let's go where it's warm instead of clogging up the church steps."

"Bye." Monica elbowed him in the ribs before bolting.